Pleasure City
Sexy
Stories
Collection

VOLUME 47

5 EROTIC SHORT STORIES

ERIC RESHER

Pleasure City/ Eric Resher. -- 1st ed.
Xplicit Press, an imprint of TLM Media LLC

ISBN-13: 978-1-62327-578-5
ISBN-10: 1-62327-578-4
eISBN: 978-1-62327-628-7

Printed in the United States of America

CONTENTS

1 TRACKING DOWN HER CITY SLAVE

My lover has run off again. This is the first time he ran out of the state, though. I'm searching for him, two states from our home at a BDSM hotel party he wanted to attend. I told him the rules. Every woman must have rules when it comes to men or they will walk all over them. I said, "Since you're my slave boy submissive, you listen and are committed to me. If you want to leave our relationship just ask. Furthermore, you need to fuck when I want. And unfortunately for you, Dante, Fem-Doms don't really fuck their submissive all that often."

I gave him sex once a month. I whipped and bound him. I took him out to fetish parties once a month. I used his body as a toilet slave. He liked that best. We played using ropes and belts and whips. I make him serve me, cleaning house, cooking, washing my clothes. Dante's a great cook. No Fem-Dom should have to cook her own food, that's beneath her.

Describing the heart of our relationship, it's love. He loves me. I'm the best mistress he's ever had. I have treated him fair. I looked after his every need. I took care of all his finances. When he wanted to go to a party, the movies, buy new submissive clothes, or books, reading up on bondage and discipline, I did all that for him. So why does he like to prove he's an individual every once in a while? That's so annoying in a submissive, especially a male.

In these hotel ballroom fetish parties, you see all types. Everyone comes into BDSM really as voyeurs at first. The sights are amazing and strange. One sight that caught my eye tonight was a cute boy of twenty, in black leather briefs, a white towel stuck in his pants, following behind his mistress and her blonde, wavy haired submissive. The submissive looked so sweet. She wore the craziest outfit. Whipped cream. Her bra and straps consisted of a heavy coating of whipped cream. The kind you put on top of a cake. Since the woman's skin had a slight olive tone, the white whipped cream stood out. Everyone noticed her. Her mistress thanked everyone for the compliments on her submissive's outfit as she led her submissive around by a dog chain attached to her right wrist's cuff. The submissive smiled. The submissive's panties were made of whipped cream too! She walked and took tiny little steps, and this is where that cute boy following behind the female pair came in. Every time the submissive woman walked, a little whipped cream came off her white whipped cream thong panties. The boy followed behind and replaced any whip cream that dropped to the floor. He also used that white towel tucked into his leather pants briefs to wipe any cream that fell to the hotel ballroom floor.

I stood watching them. Everyone parted the ballroom floor letting them pass. I broke my eyes from that food show and kept looking for Dante. I'm 5' 8" tall. In my biker boots, I'm a good 6'. So I see over the spectators and show-offs easily. I looked far into the scene of people, too. That's when a young blonde girl with straight hair noticed me.

"You look lonely. You want a new slave? I can be that slave submissive for you."

She was a hottie in a small package, only 5' 2" tall.

"Listen," she said standing right in my

path. "I have this," she measures her hands apart some ten inches. "This ten-inch dildo back at my place." She lowered her eyes and looked up again, catching mine. "I'll be your slave," she ran her long pretty black fingernail painted digits up my arm. "Let's blow this BDSM party scene and get a real bondage and submission game going."

I'm not impressed. I'm still glancing around for Dante.

She said, "I'll let you fuck the shit out my tiny pussy using that monster, only make me your submissive—forever. Forever!"

I smiled. "I like a person who makes commitment, too bad you are female."

"I can cut my hair! I can do that page boy look!"

"Nah. Women like drama."

"Like your slave boy who ran off, across the fucking state," the smirky snarl came from her black painted thin lips.

"How'd you find out about, Dante?"

She ran her other forefinger up my other arm. She twisted her petite body from side to side, "When a good mistress needs a new submissive, word gets around."

"You've got some spunk, kiddo." I sized her up with my eyes. She weighed about 100 lbs. Her long straight blonde hair gave her a hard edge though. She had tattoo stars across the left side of her lower belly for some reason. It's a shame because it sort of lowered the value of her flawless pale white skin. She wore black and white circle-stripped thigh-high stockings, black platform heels, and black tiny star earrings dangled from her lobes. Her black-halter top covered only a handful of boob flesh, but still she had style. She wore a thin black collar. Her black and blue schoolgirl skirt shouted "spank me I'm ready."

"Just let me follow you. I'll run after your motorcycle."

"You can keep up?"

"Heck yeah."

"Let's go outside." I pushed and weaved my way out of the crowded BDSM party. They didn't allow smoking in the hotel, but the booze flowed freely. A huge burly guy stood directly in my way, a little tipsy. He stared at me for a second. I raised my black studded leather wrists cuffs. He stepped aside and let us pass by him.

I led the wannabe female Goth chick into the parking lot. "There's my motorcycle, 2007 Kawasaki ZX-6R with the large seat, pink mud guards and gas tank."

Submissive Goth chick darted before me, pointed to my machine's high window shield.

I nodded. "Yeah, that's the correct one."

She started running beside it, panting, "I told you I could keep up." A wide smile cracked across her black-painted lips.

I lowered and shook my head, "You've got wit, Goth chick," I said, sauntering up to her.

"I told you I could keep up. Now take me back to my place and make me your girl."

"Not so fast." I threw my right leg over my motorcycle, clicked around, pulled the key out from the side of my black biker leather pants and revved the engine. "I got to go Goth chick." I pulled off slowly.

Submissive Goth chick kept running beside my motorcycle. I stopped.

She stopped.

I started rolling again down the long dark parking slot dotted with lamplights, empty beer cans scattered around, and the smell of weed permeated the atmosphere. I roll again, further a good ten feet.

Goth chick panted beside me.

We neared the end of the parking lot. I saw the open street clear of traffic ahead. When I stopped the smile on her face grew wider. "Cute."

"You'll take me, train me?"

I surprised her and started to take off for good. Submissive Goth chick figured my plan, she ran beside my motorcycle moving faster and faster down the last space of hotel parking lot like some kind of girl trying to make the boy's football team, one-half step behind me. I didn't turn back; I yelled, "So long Goth chick."

Goth chick hopped on the back of my motorcycle and held on tight to the passenger restraint handle like a raccoon using its claws. We both tore down the empty city street zipping pass red lights.

"I never promised to keep running alongside your motorcycle my mistress."

"Mistress Monica," I said and laughed. "I like a smart submissive, someone who can take care of herself."

She pointed out the way to her apartment complex. "I'm not like that runaway boy or yours, eh."

"Boys have to prove themselves." I revved up the handle bars, did a low wheelie. We went faster. "Everybody needs to prove their worthiness. It's the only way he knows how to impress a mistress."

"That's because he doesn't have a pussy," Goth submissive said, in a confident tone. "If he had a pussy, all he'd have to do is let his mistress have it."

"You may have a point. A dick isn't like a pussy. Dick can be fickle and wander around."

We arrived at her place. Inside, Goth chick didn't even bother to offer me a beer or glass of wine. I didn't ask. She always meant what she said. She brought me here to fuck her pussy using that ten-inch pussy breaker. She walked to her kitchen table and pressed her messages. Her former mistress made it official. "I'm getting married to Mike," the short message said, "I'm quitting the BDSM scene."

"Fucking quitter! Quitter! Quitter liars get her!"

"Yeah, yeah," I said. I did Goth chick a favor and clicked the message machine off. I pressed her hips to the wooden kitchen table ledge.

Goth chick laughed. She swung her arms wildly and pushed everything off the kitchen table. She turned around and laid back, her thin black-and-white-striped stocking legs spread wide, her blue and black tiny square school skirt around her waist. I saw her black small panties and the tiny pinks stars on them. She had this major thing about stars. She raised her legs really quick and lowered her damp panties off her butt, thighs, calves, and platform-black shoes. You'd think as fast as she runs, she'd have cheetahs or roadrunners all over her outfit and body. Goth submissive tossed the panties away like they offended her. "Do me now, Mistress Monica. Make the pain go away!"

Tempting sight, she was. "I recall you

mentioning a monster plastic cock."

Goth chick pointed to a small nightstand in the living room by her music system. I paused, eyeing her while Goth submissive stared up at the ceiling like she waited on her GYN. Her pussy flower began unrolling from that tight lily formation, as the petals of her wings grew and lengthened. I caught a scent of earth and strawberries. Her thighs showed sheens of clean sweat from running in the parking lot. Her pussy became wetter and wetter as I stared at it. I broke my mesmerizing view from her flowering cunt.

Goth chick knew how to move a situation along. She pulled me into her life, her running talents, her apartment, her spread legs, and now her pussy wings. I went over to her nightstand.

"Top drawer."

The drawer seemed stuck for a second. I used a little more muscle, and it slid open. I stared in disbelief. Goth chick had every size, length, and circumference and make of strap-on dildos in that drawer. They all lay scattered across one another. Some glowed florescent green, red, royal blue. Regular colors of black, yellow, green, blue and pink dildos accompanied the wild colors. So many different sizes my eyes had to adjust to find ten inches out all the other hundreds of inches in that treasure fuck chest. I moved them around like they were quarters or half-dollars all saved up and one was a collectable. "You've got a talent for collecting, Goth chick. You should move on from dildos to quarters and half-dollars."

"I might do that!" Goth chick snapped, the sad disbelief of being dumped by her last mistress still lingered in her voice.

I pulled out one strap-on dildo, raised it up for her to see from supine position on the table, "What the fuck is this one for?" The tiny dildo measured only one inch in length and a quarter inch in circumference.

"Oh!" She paused. "I started sex young!" She shrugged her shoulders.

"You found..."

"No my big sister gave me that, or rather I found it in her drawer. She apparently used it to practice giving anal sex to her boyfriend."

"She'd need something bigger than that."

"It fit me perfectly."

I pushed around. "Got it." I pulled the monster cock out, and it took almost a minute for the thing to release itself from the entangled other assorted cocks in that drawer. I walked back to submissive Goth chick.

"Damn that's a monster...I'm not sure."

"A deal is a deal," I reminded her.

She spread her legs wider.

"On the floor, all fours."

"You're commanding and naughty. I like that."

"Place your elbows on the floor, next to your knees."

"Like this?"

What a tempting sight she made. If I was a guy, I would have fucked her without any fanfare or lubrication. I faced facts; she had enough girly lube already dribbling down her sweaty thighs.

She pointed to the mess tossed down from the table. "Use those plastic twist ties and scissors."

I knew what she wanted.

"Bind my feet."

"Nah. I do this my way or no way, Goth chick. My rules."

"Yes mistress."

I found the bathroom, grabbed two bath towels from her shelf and took one plastic twist tie and looped it around her left elbow and the back of her left knee. Then I repeated this procedure on right elbow and knee. "Secure."

"Kinky different. Secure. Pound away."

I positioned the ten-inch strap on around my waist. I pressed against her wings and slipped right in one inch.

Goth chick moaned, "Damn I'm glad you know how to fuck."

I withdrew the monster cock and rubbed it up and down her fiery snatch. I let her feel the circumference of that monster bulbous cockhead, how unforgiving and relentless it was. I smeared her lubrication all over the black plastic toy. She tried to wiggle her butt cheeks. Goth chick wanted to move her arms around. I moved that fuck monster closer under her pussy and belly and pulled back her straight blonde hair. "You're one hungry whore to accept a cock this size."

"Yep. I'm a hungry whore," Goth chick confirmed, her tone becoming lighter.

"Look between your legs."

She peeked between her bound arms and legs. Her eyes adjusted to the length the toy stretched out under her pussy and belly. "Fucking huge. You're going to ruin my pussy and fuck my belly button. I might never eat again." She giggled, feeling better and returning to her old daring self.

"You get off on pushing past limits."

She did a hair flip. "That's how progress is made."

I moved back and forth, making sure the cock had enough lube. Her scent was unmistakable now. I wanted to help her. She seemed so helpless bound like that. She couldn't satisfy her raging desires. I pulled back and pushed that toy two quick inches inside her pussy.

Goth chick groaned. Her pussy lips spread wider, because her hips couldn't move around to accommodate the size. I saw her asshole puckering and moving in and out. Once she got used to the two inches, I moved in further another two inches.

She surprised me. Her gobbling pussy poured out lube all around that fuck monster. Her tight pale butt seemed so tempting. Her coral-pink pussy showed remarkable resilience. It's hard for a woman to see her own pussy fucking. When she gets in a Fem-Dom scene with a female, that firsthand experience usually is reserved to male (namely fucking a female) if possible. Goth chick's pussy did tricks I had never seen before. She self-lubed the black plastic barber pole moving deeper inside her tiny nook. I didn't let up. I moved down further. "You've got a good eight inches now."

"I'm deeper than that."

I pulled out and she wailed. "Fucker! Quitter. Liars get her."

"Shut up whore!" I said, "This is my scene." I slapped the dildo under her pussy again, banging it against her clit. Her clit formed a perfect stem to her pussy flower. Her thighs quivered. Her small boobs hung suspended in the air. I pressed my leather groin on her butt checks to rub the slick cock over her tiny nipples. Then I pulled back and stuffed all eight inches in her fast and furious.

"Pound that pussy!" Goth chick yelled.

I began to pound and fuck her pussy. Her small 5'2" body rocked back and forth. Her legs and arms kept her steady. I placed my hands on her hips and pressed, pressed that pussy probe deep as it could go, each time I pulled back and fucked into her another inch of plastic. Then finally, we hit pay dirt.

"You've hit the jackpot."

I kept fucking her. She worked her pussy and asshole to my rhythm. She made all kinds of babbling indiscernible new words about fucking and pussies and cocks and cumming. Goth chick's clit grew large and on my outstroke, back nine inches, I saw her pearl peeking out under the hood of flesh at the apex of her sex. The woman had an elephant pussy. Something in me felt sympathy for Goth chick because of her trick pussy. This is the kind of woman who astonished you so much, you just can't believe it. Men seeing her sword swallow all that plastic probably stopped looking at porn. You've seen it all when you see a woman fuck ten inches of meat, plastic or live.

I knew her orgasm neared because that dildo monster kept pushing back against my hip. Her pussy muscles pushed the monster out and sucked it back in. I held on tight and started pounding my hips faster, harder. I doubled my stroke pace. I double pumped inside her slick ooze, forcing out her hot juices around that monster before plunging it back into her sexual depths. Then she yelled out, "I'm cummmming. I'm fucking going to die, that monster feels so good! Faster. Push. Hump that little tiny pussy. Show that pussy clam who the boss is!"

I grabbed her arms above her elbows and rocked her entire body on that monster, giving her no room to relax. Her passion came over her and spilled out of her pussy in a massive squirt that wet the entire carpet. When I stopped, I thought about it. "That's why you like the table." I said cutting her plastic ties using the scissors.

"Yep. I tend to squirt some."

"Some. You're fucking Niagara Falls down there."

"Does that mean you're going to keep me as your submissive?"

"Yeah," I said.

I helped her clean up. While she took a bath, washing her dildo monster out first, then her body, I said, "Dante isn't getting enough sex."

"That the trouble with boys."

"Now, I'm his mistress. He's not supposed to fuck me." I stared into Goth chicks medium brown eyes. Her wet hair lay back all over her head. She looked like a swimsuit model coming out of the ocean onto the beach. Her bunny tattoo came into focus on her upper right shoulder. Then I paused and nodded.

Goth chick hesitated. "I'll fuck him in your place—to keep him around." She playfully splashed the water a bit with her pink towel.

"That's the idea."

"On one condition."

"I'll make a concession."

"I dominate him after he fucks me!"

Goth chick's offer seemed fair to me. Dante running off for more pussy deserved such a deal. "You got a deal." I helped Goth chick dry off. She told me her name was Samantha. "We have a deal, Samantha."

Dressed in another schoolgirl outfit, red and black circle striped thigh high hoses, and black flats and a gray and black mini skirt, Samantha and I hopped on my motorcycle to find Dante.

"I know where he might be."

"How do you know?"

"Because he's my brother's best friend!"

Silence.

"Yep." Goth chick said, holding on tight to my waist as we tore down the highway to the next state over. "He thinks he's safe because no one knows him in this BDSM scene."

I kept thinking what a shame to be a boy, so fucking sex crazed for girls. "Every

BDSM scene talks to the others."

"I know, but when you're a boy starved for free pussy," she pointed to the exit sign, "You do all kinds of stupid things."

We arrived at small house in an exclusive neighborhood.

She giggled. "Doesn't look like a BDSM scene does it?"

"No it doesn't."

"It's not one." She lifted her legs flashing anyone miles around in her mini school skirt. "It's my home."

Goth chick went inside. The lights were all out. First, the living room light came on. Then the kitchen, and then a few minutes later, the upstairs bathroom light. Finally, the bedroom light. An argument broke out. It sounded like Goth chick and some boy yelling and arguing. Then a second later, the bedroom lights went out and all the other lights clicked off in the same order.

Their house door opened and Dante stumbled out, pushed by Goth chick, smiling at me but snarling at him. "Found him!"

"Dante?"

Dante casts his eyes down sheepishly. "What the fuck!"

"He thought I was lying," Goth chick

Samantha said. She giggled. "I mean what I say, fucker." She pointed her black fingernail forefinger, pushing him towards me.

The two submissives stood before me. I didn't know how to get them home though. "Dante, if you want to stay you can. Just let me know you're done with the scene."

"Yeah, prick," Samantha said. "My mistress dumped me last night. Just be honest fucker."

"I just needed a break...I wanted some freedom. Freedom to fuck."

"So you came here? Two states away to fuck?"

"I've been fucking Samantha for years. She's a safe fuck. Only this time—"

"I wasn't home!"

"You said you'd be home! You promised. Liar, quitter, liars get her!"

"Shut your mouth, Dante. Shut your mouth. That's my saying, not yours!"

"Lower your voices," I had to be the adult between the two of them.

Dante turned to Samantha, "If the shoe fits."

"I'll show you my shoe when we get home, Dante," Samantha boasted.

"What does she mean?"

"We made a deal, Dante. Samantha and I."

"What kind of deal?"

"If I found you, and I did, you have to become my submissive."

"No. Noooooo. I need sex."

"Dante," I stopped him using my lower voice tone. "You came here for sex. Came to Samantha for sex? You can have her sexually as my submissive. You both are submissive to me. When you want sex, Samantha is submissive to you. The deal is after you have sex with Samantha, here, you become her submissive." I waited.

He stood there between us two women. His mind raced back and forth. He had no reason to turn down the deal.

"Take or leave it, scum," Samantha said.

"What's it going to be, Dante?"

"Do you love me, Mistress Monica?"

"Why would I go two states away, trolling around BDSM parties all night if I didn't love you?"

"I don't know. I just thought..."

"Thought what?"

"You only needed a flunky, submissive boy as your housekeeper. You can get one of me anywhere."

"I pay for everything we have together, Dante. And no, I cannot get one of you anywhere. You're unique."

"Sure. Yeah, but I sometimes forget." His blue eyes looked up to me. "I don't want to forget, but I forget all you do for me. I think...I'm useless except for what

19

you want to use me for."

"We use each other, Dante." I said calmly. "It's always been like that."

Samantha turned her brown eyes to me and pulled a lock of her straight blonde hair behind her ear. "I explained that to him."

"We'll be a family together, Dante."

"Yeah, a family," Samantha giggled.

"You really taking on Samantha? She can be lots of drama."

"I'm only drama when I'm not wanted."

"Like you caused all this drama, Dante? That kind of drama, Dante?"

"I guess I caused you grief didn't I," he admitted sheepishly.

"You just don't know." I waited. "But otherwise, I might not have met Samantha here, if I didn't go looking for you. So it all worked out in the end."

"Not in the end," Samantha said. "We'll have to see if he submits after fucking me."

"Let's go. Dante hop on. You too, Samantha."

"I'm riding next to my mistress," Dante blurted out insecurely.

"Fine. I know Mistress Monica loves me. I'm secure."

Dante fixed us a big nice meal. Then we

all retired to my dungeon and Dante laid Samantha on her back. He then positioned himself between her small legs.

"I can't take such a huge cock, Dante." Samantha pleaded.

I sat in my big chair with the high-rounded back making it clear I was the boss of these two. I laughed, as I knew there wasn't a large cock Samantha couldn't take.

"You fucked me how many times—?"

"Last month or this month?"

Dante entered Samantha. They didn't fuck like enemies. They fucked like friends, fucked like lovers. I began to wonder just how long they had been fucking one another. They knew how to pacify each other's needs. More than that, Dante moved his hands all over Samantha like he wanted to please her immensely. I watched him pump into the hilt, his balls dragging against her small white ass. Then he rose up further, squashing Samantha's cunt and pee hole and put pressure on her tiny clit. He did this five times in a row. Samantha squealed like a virgin finally cleared enough of pain to feel the pleasure of lovemaking for the first time. They hugged and kissed too.

Then it dawned on me. Dante loved Samantha, but she pulled the strings in their relationship. She might have married him, but didn't want to for some reason. I needed to find out what that reason was. Was it because she needed a new mistress? Me? Was it because she didn't want Dante to lose me? I let them fuck.

Samantha used her bare feet on his buttocks over and over again. Patting and rubbing it like her feet were hands. She rolled her hips under him. She arched her back. Her motions sucked in Dante's modest seven-inch cock, and one and half-inch circumference. She made him feel bigger than he actually was. She never let him rise up and pound her sweet pussy. I don't think Dante wanted to pound her pussy. He seemed content to stay as close to her skin-on-skin as possible. Each pore of his breathing skin next to each pore of Samantha's breathing skin. He stroked her hair. He licked her chin and lips. He kissed her eyes, nose, and ears.

Samantha remained quiet. She didn't taunt Dante with her true pussy size. She gave him a respect he desperately wanted from a woman. Although I gave him a different kind of respect, he needed this sexual respect from Samantha, too. She pushed her small breasts up to him. She begged him to suck her small titties. She said his slow entry and exits drove her mad in lust.

Dante loved to fuck slowly. That's a rare quality in a guy. Dante understood female biology. The time required to adjust to a different cock, meant a world of wonder to a woman. He braced one arm down beside Samantha and rocked his hips sideways into her tight ooze. Her liquids started flowing all over the place. He took his hand, wiped her cunt juices on his hands, and licked them off. Then he kissed her. They both loved the way she smelled. He raised her up on his thighs. She willingly turned around on her side. Together, they fucked like that gently and slowly. Rocking back and forth. Dante slipped his hand under Samantha's slippery gushing pussy. He picked up more of her greasy oils on his hand. He then pushed his thumb up her butt hole.

"You're so fucking big back there, Dante."

"You can't stand my girth."

"Have mercy on my poor butt hole. I'm a small Goth girl."

They went on like that, having strange lovey-dovey sex talk, his thumb up her butt hole rocking back and forth until finally Samantha screamed out her orgasm. Then Dante screamed out his and came with her. They relaxed and finally sat up.

"Don't move you, Drama King!" Samantha suddenly shouted. "Stay on your hands and knees. I'm going to deal with you."

He squealed, "No. No. Don't, I'll be

good."

"You will be good," Samantha suddenly turned back to me and smiled. "Where's your pink riding crop?"

I pointed to the wall.

Samantha rushed over there, her huge pussy still dripping Dante's love juices. Dante for his part stayed lying down on the soft bed, his tight butt cheeks and legs together.

She came back over and swished the crop a few times over his butt and upper thighs. "You'll listen to me next time, Dante." She brought the crop down on his butt hard. Soon he had several welts on his ass. Samantha then straddled his ass and facing me, backwards to Dante's head, she started whipping his lower calves and thighs. "He's very sensitive on these parts."

Dante made what looked like real screams of pain, but Samantha kept wailing on him. She rode up and down on him almost like he was a horse. Her hips bounced off his ass, pressing his spent dick down into the mattress. She leaned forward and hit his toes. She smiled and moaned after each smack.

I sensed tremendous relief and pleasure in her punishing Dante. She really liked being the dominate one. A Fem-Dom. Of course, the best Fem-Doms come from the best submissive. It's a cliché, but true.

She spread Dante's legs and gave his inner thighs slaps using the crop. She even slapped his drained balls one time. That brought a real leap from Dante. I started to intervene, but I noticed Samantha easing up. She delivered the one blow she wanted. That on his balls, to show Dante she wasn't to be bartered for easily. She practically already won Dante over and that's the hardest thing for a Dom–submissive relationship to achieve.

He wanted to marry her but she didn't want to settle down, the way Samantha commanded their relationship. It is inevitable; Dante and she will marry— someday. It's only a matter of time and when. That will be just fine, as long as the two of them invite me to their wedding. As long as the two of them stay submissives to me and my desires, all is good.

2 EARTHLY MOTEL SEX

Prologue

"I'm a whore! You think I'm a whore!" I said to my roommate, Cindy, as I paced back and forth in the seedy Motel No.3, near Truck Stop No.4. "Hey, hey! I like my pussy eaten! And Jake knows how to eat pussy. Jake ate pussy like a girl. I'm not giving that up, No. No. No." I started pacing again. I'll tell you how Jake ate my pussy later though. I stomped my cowgirl ankle boot on the floor, crushing a roach. I thought hard. I'm in sales. It's my job to catch clients in lies or truths in order to persuade them I'm right. The problem was Jake and I dated just two months so far. And Jake Hansomer possessed the most fickle, naughty fantasy mind; the most earnest aural perceptive ears; and the most

incendiary, intoxicating, cunt itching husky personality and body ever known to a sexual hot-blooded woman! I needed to find him and catch him. He mentioned Las Vegas on the cell phone. He loved all this cat and mouse, hide and seek travel adventuring. He's a trucker after all. He's an air elemental. Jake's been riding the roads since he turned twenty-one and legally allowed sexually bother every available girl in fifty states. He's thirty-one now. He saves his money. I wanted to sob. Curses wanted to fall from my lips. Come on Danielle. You're better than this.

Following Jake was hard, even though I could teleport myself and Cindy anywhere. I didn't know which motel out of the several he might stop at. Cindy, my bloodhound, sat on the couch. As a water elemental, she could follow any scent. I gave Cindy a pair of my worn panties, and in this way, we knew which motel to check and see where Jake's trail lay.

"I'm just saying, Danielle," argued Cindy, my blonde pretty green-eyed roommate, while she tapped out a single cigarette from the small plastic package, and then remembered she quit. She dropped the offending narcotic stick to the floor and stomped it out. "You've fucked six different guys in three days at three truck stops." She raised her feline fingers in the air three times. "Six guys!"

I pointed to my gorgeous figure, B-sized pendulous boobs. "Can I help it, Jake, ran off with every pair panties I ever had?" I fumed. I permitted myself a withering stare in the mirror in the dingy motel. I had a temper. And snatching my panties always irritated me since my college days and fraternity's frequent panty raids on our all-female dorm.

"Calmmmmmm down," Cindy lowered her hands together over her lap. "Remember your temper, Danielle."

Yes, I had a temper. But honestly, I can only say it came from fickle guys. Guys who took my heartstrings, cut them, and ran off back into the wide world without acknowledging my love for their hearts or accepting my desire for their hot-hard cocks. I sat down on the bed beside Cindy. "He's . . .he's wanking himself off at my expense, Cindy." I twisted my metal-diamond steel cowgirl cuff links. My pink cowgirl shirt stretched tight across my melon-shaped boobs. I burned my bra long ago. Nipple peaks formed a line across the cotton material. My skintight jeans held the shirt snug below my slim waist. Nothing held my fiery cunt except the rough material of the jeans forming a camel toe in my crotch whenever I sat down. "I can't let him do that to me. I'm a human being, Cindy, not a whore. When I catch up to him...Oooooogrrrrr! I'm going to...I'm going to..." I pulled on my long black curly hair.

"Fuck him again?" Cindy added dryly, crossing her legs. She now started applying black lipstick to her plump lips.

I nodded quickly twice. "Yeah! Right!" I hopped up and paced the dirty stain motel carpet floor again. "Then he's going to marry me!" I stopped and pointed an accusing finger at Cindy. "I don't do rejection as well as I fuck. So yeah. He's going to marry me, Cindy. I need stability, to settle down into something."

"Danielle, he belongs to the air elementals. You to the earth elementals. You want him to settle down. He wants to be free as quote on quote a bird."

"I don't believe in all that elemental stuff. Our grandmoms tell us that "elemental" stuff to keep us in line. If I could simply pop around faster, teleport two times a day. But I'm of the earth elementals, not air. I have to wait at least one day per teleportation. See how limiting that is, Cindy. You're a water elemental. You should understand Jake, right. You feel. He thinks."

Cindy slouched a bit on the couch. "Regardless of my elemental status, I'm not about to go behind my best girlfriend's back and fuck her boyfriend." She paused to look and read her horoscope in the paper, "Earth elementals feel, Air elementals think. Water elementals feel, Fire elementals think. So while you're *feeling all this passion, Jakes thinking about what to do about it. Frankly, he's not even sure how much you love him."*

I sat down on the couch. Cindy always had a way of calming me down. *"OK. How do I talk to him and explain my feelings?"*

Cindy put down the paper for a second, "Write him a letter."

"I hate writing."

"Unless it's a check to buy something." Cindy gave a demure giggle. *"Sing him a song. Earth signs love music."*

"That sounds corny. Besides, I'd have to write the lyrics first."

"Send him a text message."

"Uggggg writing again. Whatever happen to hugs and kisses? Touching and snuggling?"

"We live in an air age and the age of Aquarius, Computers, and Internet."

Motel No. 1, Truck Stop No. 2

Cindy didn't believe me because I'd fucked Charlie at Motel No.1, Truck Stop No.2, two nights ago. I always keep my word. I need to feel things, people, and yes, a few bodies pressed on my hot body. Those hot bodies pressed on top of me provide comfort. The ones I pressed down on reminded me I'm a live hot-blooded woman. There is nothing like the pleasure of listening to your man's breathing while you're sleeping next to him—nothing like the touching of naked sides beside one another while you sleep in the cold wet spot of the bed. I love to hear music and buy sensual attractive clothing. Clothing provides stability and understanding.

Motel No. 2, Truck Stop No. 3

And I did a nice three-way fuck one day ago at Motel No.2, Truck Stop No.3. I felt good about that free fuck. If I'm getting dumped by Jake, I might as well fuck. I'm a free girl again. Cindy took each man's $50 dollars. My knees then straddle John no.1. I reached back and stuck his seven-inch cock up my hot pussy growing wetter by the minutes. Then John no.2 came and kneeled behind me. I reached back as Cindy handed me the KY-gel, took the tube, and lubed up John no.2's dick so much; he looked like it was wrapped in Italian salad dressing. I gave John no.1 a deep kiss that bent my ass at the proper angle for John no.2 to slip deep into my hot ass. I wanted each of them. I got John no.2 in my ass real good and tight. No one was going to slip out and get away. I pride myself on giving a good fucking delivery. John no.3 only wanted a blowjob. Perfect for me—a free girl. So he stood there with his hairy skinny legs wanking off a six-and-a-half-inch pretty cock. I swallowed, stirring up saliva in my mouth, and gulped him down. I grabbed his ass cheeks, because he acted all shy. "Come here, you shy boy," I cooed to him. Of course, the thirty year old, bearded trucker resembled a boy some twenty odd years ago, but you have to stroke a man's ego before you can stroke his cock with your mouth sometimes. Then the four of us went hunting for passion in stuffed, tight places, namely, my 32C 26 32 cowgirl-model body. I never felt so good with all those cocks working away, drilling for love oil inside my caverns of lust. I moan out my passion. I screamed out my orgasms. I made all four men join me in a cacophonous of passionate yelling.

Motel No. 3, Truck Stop No. 4

Then tonight, I did an orgy at Motel No.3, Truck Stop No.4 - our current motel. Each time, those long hot cocks entered my lonely pussy, I longed to be fucking fickle, scared-ass Jake. Each time, my heart registered emptiness after my orgasms passed into my memory banks. I loved stripping for guys. Usually, stripping for the guys led off my sexual fantasy fucks. I loved lowering my skimpy panties past my knees to my bare feet. My pussy quaked when my pouty pussy lips came into view from under the silky, cotton, and satin wet stained cloths.

Surges of unbelievable lust compelled me to take on more than one man. Only

Jake satisfied me. Only Jake's woman-like pussy eating could make me stay at home and become a good homemaker; and possibly a good mother. I met Jake at a motel two months ago. He knows what I do when I'm bored and lonely. Where was Jake? My pliant tits and wet pussy yearned looking for answers I simply did not have. I fucked six more guys in anger. "I'm glad you're keeping the man-count on the conservative side, Cindy."

"Oh sure," she said popping chewing gum in her mouth as she fixed me a cup of hot tea. "I feel for you and every woman or girl who is afraid she's going to be called a slut sooner or later."

I propped my feet up on the scratched up coffee table. "Air signs must like quickie sex or sex in back alleys or in airplanes or something."

"They want sex through mental activities or similar intellectual situations."

"In English please, Cindy."

"Sex through reading erotica or from mental fantasies and sex in libraries or schools."

Motel No. 4, Truck Stop No. 5

After we gulped down the tea, we started chasing Jake down again. We teleported again. Traveling at night gave us a chance to catch Jake. We landed at

Motel No.4, Truck stop No.5. I flashed an old picture ID of Jake to the rental guy. "Seen him."

Rental guy pointed to building no.6.

When Cindy and I get there, we knock on the door. No one is in. We asked for the key. "I'll rent it to you for the night."

"How about for fifteen minutes?"

"That'll be $10."

"We're getting closer, Cindy." I held up a pair of black roses on pink satin hipster panties. I never even wore them yet. The price tag hung limp on the back. "These cum stains must be one day dry." I held the rank panties full of man jism upside down. "The big yellow stains on the white cotton crotch hinted at a man positively desperate for some real pussy. Jake's getting desperate."

"Let's hope he doesn't find some $20 whore to satisfy his urges before you catch him."

Motel No. 5, Truck Stop No. 6

"We're getting closer, Cindy." I held up a pair of blue and pink stripped Victoria Secret silk panties, my favorite from college. "These smaller cum stains almost dripped." I shook the dirty panties downward and upward like a yo-yo. "Ha! He's fucking desperate for me. And he's nearly out of cum."

Cindy shook her head pathetically.

"You're obsessed, Danielle."

"I'm not obsessed. Efficient." I said placing the dirty pair of panties in my plastic sandwich bag in my purse with the other dirty panties. "A man should have a relationship with a real woman, not some fetish relationship with her panties." I began canvassing around the room with Cindy. I noticed a road map of Las Vegas in the trashcan. "So he's ditch the Las Vegas trip."

"No Elvis wedding for you, Danielle." Cindy cracked one of her rare smiles.

"They do quickie marriages in California, too, I hope." I pointed and held up the metro road atlas. "Jake circled Los Angeles."

Motel No. 6, Truck Stop No. 7

We teleported to the Motel No. 6, Truck Stop No.7, and I flashed his ID and the rental guy said, "He stepped out for pizza."

"I'll wait for him." Cindy and I walked to building no. 5. Luckily for us no.5 building curved around a bend. Sitting in some shadows gave Cindy time to use her expired old credit card to open the door. "Hurry let's get inside. He might be wanking off to another pair of your precious panties."

We went inside. "I don't know why you came, Cindy, if you're not going to support me."

"I'm hurt! I'm hurt!" Cindy reached into her purse for a cigarette and then pulled out the plastic package. She opened the top and then frustrated threw the entire pack out the motel window. "I'm here for you, Danielle. I love you, too."

I stopped. I stared at Cindy carefully. I softened my hard search-and-find expression and opened my arms. "Come here, Cindy." I said. "I'm sorry. Give me a hug."

We hugged and held each other for a long time. The quiet time felt good and nice. I separated us and held her at arm's length like the recalcitrant child: "I must find a man. Being with a girl is good and cozy and all...but there's nothing like a man to make your ovaries jump and tumble down the old tubes to the great melting pot in your red wet womb." I stopped and gave her a meaningful "you understand" look. I smiled. I nodded yes to encourage her to agree with me.

"Okay, Danielle, you man-obsessed, girl." We gave each other a happier embrace. "Does this mean I can go back to smoking?"

"Heck, no." I gave her a strange look. "Deal is a deal. You give up smoking and I'll stop obsessing over Jake."

"But you...are obsessing over, Jake." Her big green eyes reminded me of how contradictory I'd become lately.

I lied, "I'm obsessing over my panties, not Jake."

Cindy went outside to stretch her legs. Then she snorted, "He's been eating that pizza for a good two hours now."

"Yeah, you're right, Cindy." I said, reluctantly. "Let's go have a look."

"You mean teleport to the pizza place?"

"Yeah, that sounded like a great idea until I thought about it."

"Danielle, it's better to wait and surprise him." Cindy came back inside and closed the motel door.

I kept looking. The place was spotless of used panties anyway. I looked everywhere and finally plopped down on the couch. I lay my head back and dropped my hand to the back of the sofa cushion. My hand slipped into the crease and felt something damp. There was my satin black panties, lace tops, my name embossed across the front, and a huge wet stain all over the crotch and front. "Ewwwwww!" I held them up with the tips of my fingers. "Found them, Cindy!" I pushed the offending garment close to her face.

She bent backward like one of those flexi Russian gymnastics girls. "Gross, double gross."

"That's what I'm saying." I reached inside my purse and carefully placed my used panties inside a plastic bag with the others I collected. "All that good delicious cum could have been inside my cooze. My deep cunt might be swishing that cum around. My wet warm hole might be sending the nourishing man-liquid into my baby-making womb by now."

"You really want a truck driver husband, Danielle?" She canvassed around the motel for clues about his next stop onto California. "He'll be gone for long days driving around." She went into the kitchen looking for something to eat.

I sat on the bed waiting for Jake's return. Cindy sat on the small sofa. We sat around having a heart-to-heart talk about marriage. We watched some television, then viewed cable. Some porn came on showing two lonely cute women having sex. One girl wore a see-thru plastic skirt over her black leather bodysuit; the other wore a black leather minidress with black fishnet hosiery. The first lady had breasts-length slick black hair; the lady in the clear, see-thru skirt was a blonde. Cindy and I watched. We got steamed up.

"Close the blinds, Cindy."

In a flash, Cindy closed the blinds and we both got naked. I started rubbing my pussy all over watching the two California beauties in their perfect tans undress and 69 each other. Cindy, started off touching her breasts, which I thought was typical of a water elemental. We both slowly moved our hands over our bodies, legs, and tummies and put our hands up to our lips before going back to our favorite starting spot. Close ups showed the women's pretty pussies. The raven-hair woman's pussy looked like trickles of water. Her clitoris vaguely defined and long; her inner labia ran out from under a rectangular tuff of well-clipped short black hair. "I bet her pussy hairs are soft," I said.

Cindy fixated on the dark-hair beauty. Gasping each time, they showed her watery pussy. Her outer labia forming a groove like a creek bed, as the narrow inner labia lips flowed inside down toward her steamy cunt hole and ass crack. The wetness she generated accented her water-shaped pussy.

The blonde goddess wore her hair in a pretty fish braid that swept up her head toward her forehead, instead of down toward her neck. Her earthy pussy resembled the classic lily flower. Her clit distinct and visible at the top of her slit with her clitoral hood sloping down and her clit peeking out. Her outer lips high, but not as high out as her inner labia that curled in on one another like the petals of the lily flower. Once the dark-haired beauty licked them and seduced them, the blonde's inner lips unfolded like a blooming flower. "She's so beautiful," I said.

"The blonde has a pussy like mine," Cindy said.

"No way!"

"Sure."

"The black hair goddess has a cunt like mine!" I exclaimed.

"Let me see."

I threw my legs over the back of the couch.

Cindy put her face close to my sex. "You sure do."

"Show me yours, Cindy." She had a really pretty lily flower. "That's not fair. I should have your earthly cunt–"

"And you my watery cunt," Cindy finished my sentence all excited.

"On second thought," we both said. "We couldn't suck our own pussy types!"

With that, Cindy and I moved into our own 69, as the cable porn girls neared their orgasms. I laid down and Cindy threw her shorter legs over my face.

"You smell sweet and musky, Cindy," I cooed.

"You taste lovely and salty, Danielle."

Cindy kept kissing my pussy all over. She made sure every watery ridge and crease felt no neglect. She pushed her tongue all over my outer cunt lips. She nibbled and sucked in my flesh driving me so lust crazy I forgot all about Jake's hard penis. All I wanted was Cindy's soft lips rubbing and kissing and pressing against my pussy. She knew just how to treat each twisty curve of my female flesh. Jake was good, but not this good. Soon Cindy had me dripping like a leaky faucet.

I did my best to return the effort. Cindy's pussy allowed me to linger and gently take my time growing her blooming pussy. I wished the light in the motel shined brighter. Every once in a while, the cable television light blasted high, and in a flash, I saw the full beauty of Cindy's unfurled pussy flower. Her inner lips lay flat against her outer labia, down near her pussy hole. The way she opened made my tongue slurp up her juices—juices that tended to pool in her wings. I flattened my tongue and trapped all her feminine love fluids, and lifted my tongue higher and higher up her groove until; naturally, I bumped my head on into her protruding clit. How beautiful it was like a pistil sitting there in the middle of Cindy's pussy. Her pale skin made the image more intoxicating and apt. I wanted to be a porn photographer. I turned my face sideways, took her long clit between my lips, and pulled downward. It was easy from my position. Cindy lowered her pussy closer to my face as she moaned and let out a lusty expression of her appreciation of my tongue. Her inner lips flowed direct from two clear lines from her clitoral hood. It was beautiful. "I can't believe you've been hiding this pretty pussy from me all these years, Cindy."

"Yours is unique. I like how intricate you are down here." She kept dipping her head in between my stretched out legs. I wanted to close my thighs around her soft hair touching my thighs. I wanted to hump her face hard and rough. I don't know what was coming over me.

Cindy bent her knee and was able to let her pussy rest on my face. She practically smothered me with her lily pussy. I never liked gardening, but seeing Cindy's pussy gave me another reason to consider the traditional hobby. I pushed my fingers into her sex finally. Her lily responded with copious amounts of girl goo. My slick fingers went inside her, and I felt her pushing down, squeezing my fingers. It was beautiful to see my fingers retreating wet with her fluids. I loved how her pussy hole expanded and stayed open for a few seconds before closing completely. "You're a fucking virgin," I said.

"You're making me blush, Danielle."

I humped Cindy's fingers plunging in and out of my sweet sex. I must admit, I didn't have any reservations about how I looked down there, with Cindy eating my snatch. I felt free. I come to the realization, she knew how to please my pussy better than any man. She sure knew how to eat my pussy better than any man did. I felt

Cindy's thumb on my clit. Her first three fingers stuffed into my love hole. She rocked her fingers back and forth, hitting my clit, and then rowing my inner pussy ridges flat and smooth in her sexual rocking rhythm. I arched my back and humped forward on her thumb unconcerned if she thought I was horny. Yes, I was horny as a naked white woman running through an African jungle. I wanted to take on Cindy's whole hand.

And as if reading my mind, Cindy removed her thumb from my clit and curled it inside my pussy next to her three fingers. "Oh, that, Oh that...feels so good." I nearly fainted. She pumped hard and withdrew her fingers, and I felt her entire hand curved and slipped into my pussy. She balled her hand into a fist and started pumping so fast in and out; I came right away in an explosion of pussy squirting juices. I relaxed. Then Cindy pressed her breasts between my thighs and relaxed.

I wanted to show her a good time. My purse lay nearby and I reached into it and grabbed my lipstick. The lipstick shape fit a pussy. The tube was long and thick. I don't know if they designed it for a woman's private dildo, but I'd been using it for sex for some time. This freed up my hands. I wiped the tube clean just in case. I then sucked on it for good measure to lubricate the tube of prettiness. Then I slipped it into the opening of her cunt and let it sit there. The inner edges of her cunt sucked and sucked, and inch by inch my tube of lipstick disappeared into Cindy's slipper slot. Then I pulled it out before it went all the way end, the base making this really easy to do. I licked and rubbed my fingers fast around her pretty clit. I loved how her cunt kept taking that tube into its neither space, like a magic act.

"I'm coming!" Cindy groaned loudly as I brought her to a thunderous climax using my strong lips and agile tongue. We took a shower and relaxed. We felt better.

Finally, at four o'clock in the morning, Jake comes back. I heard him first. "Wake up, Cindy," I said pushing her as she lay on the bed beside me. "That's Jakes cowboy walk." Jake's tall. He's black and his black T-shirt is bulging in all the right places, his arms and chest, that magnificent six-pack I love to watch when I'm giving him a blowjob.

We run into the bathroom and hide. We wait until he opened the door, carrying in a huge box of pizza, a six-pack of cola, and bag of chips. "Let's go, Cindy."

"Trumpets or bugles are supposed to play at this point, right, Danielle?"

"We'll see. I'm going to surprise him." I said peeking out the bathroom door.

We listened carefully as Jake puts the chips on the table and held the pizza box.

He opened the refrigerator to put up his colas. I said, "This is our best time to surprise him."

I walked quickly out. Cindy followed close on my heels. The dingy carpet covered our footsteps. I know Jake hears my cowgirl boots on the kitchen floor though. I reached inside my purse while moving over behind him. "There's your stinking fetish panties, Jake!"

Our surprise didn't have the desired effect. He didn't jump or flinch. He turned around, as the bundle of dirty panties he'd masturbated on, fell over onto the opened pizza box.

I experienced a gamut of perplexing emotions. I found his nearness disturbing and exciting. Jake stared at me baffled.

"Why? I love you, Jake!"

He said calmly. "And I love you, too." He reached down and pulled the used panties off the pizza. A pepperoni stuck on the black satin panty front.

I put my hands on my hips defiant. "Why carry around my used and clean panties?"

He placed the panty on the kitchen table. "It was the only way to have you near me?"

I wasn't going to let Jake off the hook. I wouldn't let him explain away his bad boy behavior this time. "Jake, do you love me or my panties? Me or my sex-scent as you call it?"

"Both." His face was pensive.

"Then why don't you call when you stop at these seedy motels?" I had tears in my eyes.

He placed the pizza on the table. "I don't know. I figured you'd be tired or asleep. You work, too."

This wasn't headed in the right direction. I wanted us to reach the core of our relationship problems. But Jake hated yelling and screaming. He didn't like to fight. He thought it was unnecessary. I pressed on. "You know I fucked six guys out of a broken heart. I didn't want to fuck them. I needed you, Jake. But you, you only needed," I picked up my used underwear. "My used underwear! Perhaps, I should sell them to you as a going away memento."

His face finally registered some regret. He faced our situation. I could tell by his bewildered look. "I did say I loved you." He paused. He embraced me in an envelope of pure golden love.

"Do you love the woman inside—my soul? Or is it just hot sex?"

I felt him kiss me. Our loved came back a hundred fold.

"I never stopped loving your soul. That inward part of you makes me happiest to come home. It's lonely on the road. I've made some mistakes with women on the road before. That's what stopped me from marrying all this time. It warms my heart to know you're missing me."

"Why didn't you just tell me that, Jake?"

"I'm telling you now, Danielle."

I felt his flesh against my flesh, man against woman. His tormented groan was a heady invitation. I asked Cindy if she didn't mine us fucking on the bed.

"I've seen people fucking on cable all the time, be my guest."

Jake undressed me carefully and slowly. He took time to explore and arouse me like he always does. I lay panting on the bed, my huge tits heaving up and down and my head spinning, thinking about our deep found love. He took his time as I lay underneath his massive hard frame. His callous big hands swept all over my body. I tucked my curves neatly inside his own contours. I raised my chest, showing him the beauty of my big soft breasts. I taunted him. Then quickly I slid out from beneath Jake. My naked thighs grasped his own. My heated core and his hard presence found a soft union of delight. I kissed him. His hands touched lightly over my hardening nipples. We joined along our entire body.

I didn't think about Cindy. All my thoughts welcomed Jake into my body. I melted against his world. He melted against mine. The pleasure was pure and explosive. I pressed down harder and rose again and again. Sweet agony compelled my senses, my aching breasts, and my trembling thighs. I felt my every defense weakening until, until the shaking began underneath my hips. Involuntary tremors of arousal rolled over me and Jake, as we could hold back no longer. We gasped and sighed. Then we slipped into the numb sleep of satisfied lovers.

When I woke up, Cindy already had breakfast made—pizza omelets. "Jake woke up early."

"He didn't wake me?"

"You needed your sleep, Danielle. But as an air elemental, he left you this note."

"Danielle,

I want you always with me. Come follow me and meet me in Los Angeles at this address.

And I don't fuck anyone else but you.

Love you forever, Jake.

P.S. You didn't wear any panties—so I took your blue jeans you wore!"

I sighed. "I guess he is as addicted to me as I am obsessed with him."

"Mutual obsession is a good thing, Danielle, a good thing."

3 JUANITA'S EIGHT-HUNDRED DOLLAR DEAL

Juanita peeped out at the front door to her exclusive first floor, $800 a month apartment in Los Angeles. The doorbell rang again. Juanita said, "Shit, the rent man and he's early." She darted away from the peephole. She wore a $50 gray baby-doll dress, all five black buttons close covering her huge D-cup tits. Her hot pink Bali bra and panty set cost $60. Her strappy baby-doll didn't reach much lower than her $150 purple super mini-skirt did on her dark slim thighs. Her big $200 white pearl drop earrings dangled from her dark earlobes under her $70 permed straight black hair. On her feet, Juanita wore her $300 nice pair of extra-ankle straps on wooden heels. Two-inch heels of wood that looked richer than a CEO's boardroom table.

"Oh shit," Juanita said, dancing nervously in front of the door. Her outfit alone just cost $830 dollars. "I knew I should have forgotten about the party tonight. I needed to pay my $800 rent. Now Reuben Wilde is going to hassle me until the sixth."

Reuben held his dark shorthaired head down in front of the key hole. "I'm tired of standing out here, Juanita." He wore a light blue dress shirt, thin black leather belt and dark taupe colored dress pants. His short dark hair looked like a toupee he slapped on every morning. Black bangs dropped across his young thirty-five-year-old forehead. His pink skin tone seemed flush from knocking on apartment doors in the still-early April sun.

The conservative manager always came exactly on the first to collect the rent, when Juanita really had until the sixth. But Juanita thought, if I open the door like this, he's going to know I had had the rent money. "Shit. I hate his stocky white ass," Juanita muttered behind her front beige door. The huge Roman columns and full-length windows of her apartment made it impossible for her to lie and say she's not in. He had to have seen her. She didn't know if he had a beer belly under all those loosely conservative fitting blue shirts he wore. She was somewhat curious however. Why doesn't he have a girlfriend like the rest of the guys? He should be preparing to party tonight, not bother people about the rent before the sixth!

"I know you're in there. I need that rent money." He waited patiently.

Juanita got an idea. "Just a sec, Reuben...You're not supposed to be here," she started undressing right there at the door. "Not supposed to pick up the rent until the sixth of each month."

"I know. I know, Juanita. I'm a small fish in a small pond. I don't own the building. I'm simply the manager. Griffin "Slim" Gilmore owns the building."

Juanita opened the door nude. Her dark-brown skin glistened in the noon sun. One bead of sweat started from her throat and darted down between her D-cup breasts. She stood there defiantly.

"Wow!" He stared. "What the fuck!" He turned his eyes down to the floor as he tried to walk inside her apartment.

"No. No!" Juanita said. She squatted sending her heavy dark breasts bouncing on her ribcage as her 5' 4" 120 lb. figure reached the nadir and grabbed her clothes and shoes. "Here! Take it all back to the stores since you're so early for the rent money!" She stuffed her grey and purple ensemble in Reuben's white hands. "Take these $300 shoes too!" She piled them on top of her outfit, as she struggled to push Reuben out the door. "I hardly wore them around the house for three minutes!"

"I can't ...I don't know where to start returning these?" he held up the pile of women's clothes, and one of the strappy wooden shoes fell off the pile and bounced off the light brown apartment carpet. Reuben tried to not to gawk at Juanita who stood there now not even covering herself up. "Juanita..." He lifted the pile of clothes in front of his eyes, hiding his eyes. "Let's talk about this."

Juanita stepped to one side and opened the door wider. Reuben quickly stepped inside.

Juanita closed the door. She locked it. Reuben walked around, and Juanita got the impression he liked what he saw of her firm naked black ass.

Reuben apologized. "I know I'm early, but Griffin's riding my ass about people being late paying and all." Reuben picked out the baby-doll and handed it back to Juanita said, "Put this on. Let's talk."

Reuben took the pile of clothes around and put it on the long red couch in Juanita's apartment. The sparsely decorated apartment almost looked lived-in. She had only been there for six months.

Juanita shimmied the grey baby-doll over her head and down her shoulders.

She didn't even bother buttoning up the five black buttons. She showed some deep dark cleavage to Reuben. His cock started to rise in his taupe-colored dress slacks.

"If you'd come on the sixth," Juanita defended. "I was going to have the money by then. I'm meeting a client."

"You're not hooking are you Juanita? Hooking is against your lease."

Juanita put her hands on her hips, walked around the long red couch and sat on the other end. She didn't bother trying to close her legs. Reuben saw her dark charms anyway—her bald pussy. Her black pussy looked darker than the rest of her skin on her thighs, mons, and belly. Only her dark areolas matched the rich blackberry color on her cunt. Soft pink flesh inside her pussy lips flashed out at Reuben as his eyes kept dropping between her legs and bounced back up to her D-cup dark breast's flesh.

"Of course, I'm not hooking. Not like half the other white girls in this exclusive apartment building are!" Juanita blurted out. Her head bobbing, as if she was really getting angry and about to sass Reuben really good. Her baby-doll started rising up near her crotch again. Reuben could see under the short garment anyway. He even saw her dark pussy getting slick wet with her pussy juices.

"Juanita. Okay. Great!" His brown eyes

looked worried. "When will you have it?"

"Give me until the sixth like you're supposed to!" Juanita's tone became sassy. Juanita knew it would only be a matter of minutes before she started calling him some white "this" and "that." She breathed in real deep and calmed herself. Her D-cup breasts went up and down slowly. She moved her hands up and down her sides. Unfortunately, the deeper she breathed, the harder and longer her dark nipples became! She may have been calm, but her nipples stood about two inches from her goose bumped dark areolas. Her nipples had perfect circle tops.

Reuben wanted to just reach out and pinch them. "It's getting hot in here," Reuben replied and unbutton his top button on his blue dress shirt. He inadvertently grabbed his crotch.

"I can handle that for you, Reuben," Juanita flicked her brown eyes down at his crotch. Then she laughed. "Isn't this funny. I'm sitting here practically naked. You're talking about how April's hot. You're looking at all my clothes right under your nose."

Reuben laughed. "This is a riot." He lifted up Juanita's clothes and placed them closer to her side of the long red couch. He rubbed the couch's surface. "Very soft."

"I'll just put a few of these on, since I'm not taking them back yet," Juanita winked, as her legs parted while she strapped on the rich wood sole, two-inch strappy heels. Her manicured white nails accented her beautiful brown hands, and Reuben was given a first row seat to his very first black stripper act. Bending down to lock the final of four straps, Juanita's D-cup tits swayed back and forth like coconuts in the wind. Her permed black hair played peek-a-boo with her white pearl drop earrings. She stood up. Juanita turned around, showing off her strong dark brown thighs. The apartment light caught on her dark skin, defining her muscle definition.

Reuben knew Juanita kept herself in good shape. Reuben wanted to fuck her.

Juanita knew Reuben wanted to fuck her. She walked closer and then, turning once more, lifted her gray baby-doll up off her firm buttocks. The baby-doll barely covered her past her ass anyway.

Reuben whistled. Juanita spun around and straddled his lap in a second.

"Now, you were saying, Reuben...about the rent?" She kissed him, and reached down and palmed his long white cock under his dress taupe colored slacks.

He started to unbutton his blue dress shirt and return Juanita's hot kisses. He threw off his shirt. Juanita had his belt unbuckled in no time.

"Stand up, Reuben," Juanita said, admiring his modest chest, and slight belly. "You're in pretty good shape for a white man."

Juanita had his pants off and all his clothes piled on top of her clothes. She straddled his white firm thighs. "Nice and strong thighs."

"From walking all around the apartment complex."

"I love strong thighs, Reuben," Juanita said, and she smothered him again, laying her heavy tits into his chest forcing him back onto the long red couch. She fed him her dark berry nipples. His white palms grabbed both at the same time. He didn't know which one to lick first, so Juanita forced her left, slightly bigger tit into his mouth as he tried to mouth the words "beautiful."

Her long black straight hair covered his face as she looked back and grabbed his pink cock and placed it near her sex. She rocked forward slightly and then rocked back inserting Reuben into her dripping black sex. Her pink lips stretched around his pink cock. Her dark outer labia sucked his white dick into her darkness. She squeezed her internal pussy muscles each time Reuben sank in further into her cunt.

They fucked for a good three minutes.

She loved how her cunt lips clung to his

long thin cock on the out strokes.

Reuben loved how his cock forced her short inner labia wings inside her wet pussy on the in strokes. They went back and forth focusing on their own moments of internal and external pressure and pleasure. Each one silent and sensing how their white and black skin rubbed and teased one another deeper and harder, higher and more intensely. Then Reuben grunted, and he pulled out, still hard and long, and narrow. Juanita's pussy dripped some of his baby-making seed from her dark interior. She knew he had come inside her, but luckily, like most girls, Juanita used birth control.

"I might as well fuck you again, since this will not materialize $800 into my pocket," Rueben confessed.

"Fuck me doggy style," Juanita chirped. "I've never had a white man doggy style before."

They switched places, and Juanita put her knees and hands on the long red couch and turned her face back over her shoulders. She reached up and messed up Reuben's short black locks of hair. "Now you look like Elvis's younger brother."

They laughed.

"And Elvis could fuck, from what the girls in Tennessee said," Reuben added.

Reuben Wilde had no trouble finding where to place his seven-inch, narrow cock because of the dark contrasts between Juanita's outer labia and inner labia and pink pussy center. All he had to do is aim for the wet pinkness. He pushed inside her and sighed.

Juanita murmured, "Hhhhhaaaa MMMMMM! Your modest cock feels good." She stayed perfectly still and let Reuben do all the work. She looked straight ahead over the armrest of the long red couch. She looked at the door. She remembered how crazy that was, undressing and giving him her new store bought clothes to pay the rent. Now they were fucking like dogs and enjoying the time of their lives.

Juanita noticed he wore a ring, but the rumor was Reuben was single. He lived alone. He went out and came back alone. She felt confident he was single. "You can hit this twice a week, if we hooked up as a couple, Reuben?"

Reuben grunted. He grunted again. Each time he grunted, he pushed his white body forward into Juanita's soft pink flesh. His pink cock slid between her plump blackberry ass hiding her precious pink pussy folds. "I can't. Griffin doesn't want me fucking the residents."

Reuben fucked harder and Juanita matched his intensity. They both began to show perspiration along their skin. They felt their passions reaching a peak; then they both screamed, "I'm coming!"

Reuben collapsed onto of Juanita's dark brown back, and together, they lay on one another. No one moved. Their combined love juices started leaking out. Juanita reached to their pile of clothes and quickly placed Reuben's white jock shorts under her pussy to catch all their love fluids.

"That's was fantastic, Reuben!"

"Great Juanita. I missed judged you. I thought you'd be some stuck up black bitch."

"Actually, I'm Griffin's cousin!"

"Our Griffin!"

"The one." Juanita waited for the information to sink in. "Look it up on the Internet when you get home, if you don't believe little old me."

"Oh fuck! Oh fuck, fuck! I'm in trouble now!"

"Not really," Juanita said, turning under Reuben and then pulling him down to embrace her again. "You come and get the rent on the sixth every month, and I won't say a thing about this." She smiled.

"But what if Griffin asks?" Reuben said, nervously.

"What? Asks about his cousin's late rent before the sixth?"

Reuben thought about it. Reuben smiled. "He wouldn't dare ask about your rent before the sixth."

"He wouldn't dare!" Juanita nodded and placed Reuben's white hands on both her black two-inch nipples.

Reuben pinched Juanita's nipples and bent down to lick them while Juanita wrapped her legs around his waist again.

Juanita said, "Aren't you glad you didn't collect the rent on the first?"

Reuben smiled and sucked in one of her dark wrinkled nipples. He stopped. He gave Juanita a deep kiss. "I'm glad I didn't try to collect your rent before the sixth, Juanita."

"We'll keep this as our little secret, Reuben, if you suck my black pussy?"

"Wow! Yeah." Reuben rose and the long red couch made it easy for him to move back and place his white lips on her dripping sex. He rubbed his white hands all along her dark brown thighs. He traced her muscle definition defined by the apartment light and sun. He moved in slow sweeps, flowing his palms up both her thighs at the same time, toward her cunt. Then he closed in gently and pinched her dark cunt lips together. He pulled them apart. He marveled at her pink clit at the top of her dark sex.

Juanita thought Reuben knew a thing or two about pleasing a woman by the way he massaged her thighs up and down. Up and down, he moved inside her thighs and back outside her thighs; finally, Reuben narrowed and roamed his hands over her black cherry cunt lips and gracefully lightly touched her clit still throbbing. She felt him lower his mouth to her sweet pussy and lick. His tongue felt hot and juicy. He licked longer below, gathering her love nectar; he licked shorter above where her clit darted in and out of her inner labia folds playfully. Reuben began licking the middle of her cunt and down the sides. He kept up a nice good rhythm that drove Juanita crazy. She couldn't take it anymore and, finally, grabbed his dark short hair, and forced his white face to stay inside her cunt until she shuddered in her orgasms.

"Ahhhhaaaaaaa. Uuuuuggggghhhhh, Yesssssssssss! Wonderful!" Her black body went ridged and straight. Then she relaxed.

After resting ten minutes, Juanita said, "Since you can't date the resident. We'll just have to keep our first of the month fucks secret too!"

"That's not a bad idea, Juanita! I like it," Reuben said, licking her cunt fluids from his lips and fingers

"I'll be waiting on the first, nude by the front door," Juanita said and laughed.

"No problem, dark lady. No problem at all."

ERIC RESHER

4 NEW HARMONY CITY SEX CLUB

Spaceship Captain Gunter Faber of the Conestoga weighed carefully how much of his strange story in the New Harmony Space Station he should tell his superiors. The High Council of Flight Corp wanted answers. And Gunter never backed down from a fight. The fact that he was safely back on his spaceship would not satisfy them. Three thousand and forty-four people were unaccounted for – disappeared somewhere. His investigation only added two more to that number.

How did he survive?

All he remembered was her slim, sexy white body and cone dark nipples floating in space above his nude, black body as she rode his hard-as-steel cock. He contorted his body into an arch, much like a bridge, and she – this beautiful woman – stepped around, walking over his torso, her pussy never losing contact with his eight-inch-long, three-inch-circumference hot love pole.

But that didn't make any sense at all. Not in this reality, it didn't. Nor did it make sense when he collapsed on the floor and the slender woman's airplane-strip-decorated pussy stayed on his amorous and throbbing fuck tool. This enabled Gunter to thrust up inside her wet pink gash as she knelt on her knees, swinging her hips from side to side. Gunter grabbed her hips. She lifted her body and eased back down over his slick black shaft, taking his fullness in her deep, wet pussy. She loved him. She adored him; he could tell by her expressions. He sensed it, too, in his soul. Each time she took him into her body, he weakened. He gave in to her needs, wants, and desires. He longed for her when she rose off from his black barber pole before engulfing his ebony cock meat again – all juiced and slippery from her pussy juices. He wanted to stay with her forever. He listened while she moaned and whispered how perfectly they fit one another. She slammed down the full 120 pounds of her 5-foot, 6-inch-tall body, until Gunter's mind and body released his physical energy and shot gallons of white spunk up her clutching slippery cooze. All the time she was cooing, OM–AH–OO–OM–AH–OO. She touched him everywhere, frantically, before she leaned down and bit him gently on the right side of his pectoral muscles, not more than one inch from his nipple. Then she exploded in her own orgasm.

Now he sat back at the helm of the Conestoga. Six huge faces on a large flat screen stared hard at him.

"I don't know how I escaped – I – I do – but.... It should have been impossible. I should be gone like my crew, like all the others in the New Harmony City Space Station."

An old Jewish High Council member said, slowly, "Tell us what you remember."

"What I remember...." Gunter tried to recollect. "What I remember is..."

"We're going to cut loose after this is solved, Gunter," said Maria Garzia through her communication earpiece. Maria's tan wasn't poured on or sprayed on. Hispanic by birth, Maria Garzia's height reached 5 feet, 8 inches. Model material, her only beauty flaw was the heavy eyebrows she said she inherited from her grandfather, a Bolivian Indian several generations back. Gunter understood why Steve Volk always tried to get into her pants. Even though she was single, Maria wouldn't have any of that. Gunter kept his eye out for Maria.

Gunter countered, "We came here to work, not to have fun, Scientist Garzia." Gunter could party with the best of them – when he didn't have serious work ahead. That was why he hated his crew getting all excited before completing their mission. New Harmony was the third largest space station city in this part of the galaxy. Something had to be done to fix things before any more civilians went missing.

"Have fun, do some work, and kill a few aliens in New Harmony Space City. Party like Garzia said. Whooo hoooo," Steve, the computer technician, jibed around as they floated through the space lock, waiting for decontamination.

"Something isn't right here. We've been sent by the Flight Corp's High Council to find out what that is. Why – and *where* – did half of the people in New Harmony City disappear to?"

The space lock decompressed. Breathable oxygen filled up the decontamination chamber. Then the lasers started their light dance around them; the beams flowed through their suits, their skin, and their bodies. They waited a few minutes for the female computer voice to confirm what they already knew.

"All clear. No contamination."

All three took off their spacesuits and helmets, leaving them in the space dock as they walked toward the entranceway. Each wore a dull silver uniform, pants and a shirt, and combat boots.

Steve suddenly shook his head. "I –"

"What, Steve?"

"Nothing, Captain Faber. I'm good. Maybe all those people are fucking in some underground sex club." He laughed.

"You wish," scoffed Garzia as they went through the entranceway and over an arch bridge.

"Space sure looks peaceful from inside," Steve said, with a satisfied look on his face.

"Maria, I want an analysis of the atmosphere."

She reached into her bag. "Yes, sir. I think the best place to test is an area with the highest population concentration."

"There are a lot of contaminating men in the bar that we'll soon pass through," Steve laughed.

"Shut up, Steve. You think every girl wants to date a guy." Garzia gave him her hardest stare. "Sometimes a girl just wants to do science. Nothing but science, Steve."

Steve shook his head in disbelief. "Yeah, right, Garzia."

Gunter gave Steve an angry look. "Cut it out, Steve." Gunter's impeccable credentials landed him the Captain's Chair of the Conestoga. He never backed down from a proper fight and he always finished what he started.

The three sauntered over the walkway and read the blue and white sign above: Borough #1.

"This is one huge megalopolis, Gunter."

Garzia added, "Yeah, Steve, and of all places, we enter the roughest part of it first."

"Keep your cool. Keep your cool," Gunter said, as the walkway steel door opened and the hot air assaulted their senses. Loud rap music filled the air. The strobe lights twirled blue and white beams. People walked around. Some sat on tables, drinking emerald-green and florescence-yellow alcoholic beverages. Steel poles glimmered and flashed on and off in the deep background as hot strippers of all races and genders twirled around them. Someone separated the tables in front of the strippers by sex, women watching the muscular-cut men dancing in fishnet shorts, men watching the women pole dancing in skimpy leather and latex thongs and open nipple bras.

"Slow night. Not many people around. As I remember it, this place used to be hopping busy!"

"Must make you feel at home, Gunter," Maria said, pulling out her atmospheric instrument. She waved it around. She randomly measured people who walked by them.

"Both you and I, Garzia."

"Back in the old barrio-borough concrete city."

Maria and Gunter laughed.

Gunter joked, "Just because you didn't have the privilege of growing up in a slum, run-down, rat-infested city like our ancestors, Steve, doesn't give you the right to joke about them."

Steve coughed, realizing Gunter's sensitivity. "Nah, sir, no offense, but growing up in a rich neighborhood has its hazards, too: child abuse, drunken parents who don't give a damn about you, only care about the money they make. Why show the first Borough District out of five to the world?"

"Silver spoon," Maria said. "The other space docks jammed over a month ago."

"You wanted to enter Borough #5, where all the rich people live," Gunter scoffed.

"If you can live by the rich, you'll soon become rich. Even with all their strange problems."

"What a bunch of space rock," Maria said. "New Harmony's middle class is dwindling every year. Soon every borough will be like Borough #1."

"Let's head on through to the core and

talked to the mayor."

"I need to take one last temperature reading," Garzia said. "Even with all this body heat, the temperature of this place is fifteen degrees too high. Perfect for breeding bacteria."

"I heard they ran into a meteor storm recently, Gunter."

"Nah, Steve. New Harmony doesn't move, so the meteors ran into it."

"You know what I mean."

"Yeah, that might be the source of the problem."

"Sir," Maria broke in. "That's when the first disappearances began, two weeks ago."

The three of them were leaving Borough #1 when Garzia twisted her head around at something moving quickly through the air. "Did you see that, Gunter? Steve?"

"I didn't see anything, Maria."

"Neither did I. What did it look like?"

"It looked like someone or something running from the floor onto the walls. Like a parkour jumper."

Steve asked, "Did they stop and do some breakdancing on the floor?"

"I'm serious, Steve." She looked about suspiciously. "I know what I saw."

"We'll find out more when we enter the

core and see Mayor Lundquist."

"Welcome to New Harmony Space Station," said Mayor Lundquist. "You've heard of our unusual problem. Have a seat, have a seat." He gestured to three art deco chairs sitting around his metal desk.

"Isn't it hot in here?" Steve said.

"Yeah," Maria agreed.

"Well, things haven't been working so well on the ventilation side of things lately," Mayor Lundquist pulled out a white handkerchief from his suit pocket. "I might have to start working in the nude."

"That'd be against station regulations, Mayor," said Gunter and added a smile. "Tell us about the first disappearances, please, and the meteor storm."

"That storm is going to be a lot easier to explain, Captain Faber."

"Rumor says aliens came aboard."

"I'm afraid, Steve, you've been watching too many twenty-first-century sci-fi flicks. What I can tell you is that it all started in Borough #1; we think so because it has been the main entry point for so long. A male gigolo disappeared there and no one has found him yet. He's our case zero. Find out what happened to him and you may solve this case, Captain." Mayor Lundquist pressed back in his chair and stared ahead, lost for a good long minute.

Gunter, Steve, and Maria looked at him. Gunter finally waved his hand in front of Mayor Lundquist's eyes. "Mayor?"

Gunter looked back at Maria and Steve. When they turned back to the mayor, he had vanished.

"What the fuck?" said Steve.

"We better get to work right away," Garzia replied slowly.

Steve said, "We're on our own."

Gunter got up, walked around the desk, and sat in Mayor Lundquist's chair. He tried to see what the mayor might have been staring at. In front of the mayor's desk was a picture of the cyber movie star Susanno Brockel, New Harmony's own Marilyn Monroe. Gunter rummaged through his desk. He pulled out a to-do list written on a white notepad. "We've got to get some answers."

Gunter then went to a locked safe. He tried to open it. "Don't stand there, computer hacker. Get over here and unlock this thing!"

Steve strutted over after winking to Garzia. She rolled her eyes at him.

"Oh, you need my extracurricular skills now," Steve bragged. "Like I said, growing up with a silver spoon in your mouth isn't all they say it is."

"Just help us before we all disappear, Steve. Maybe it'll keep your mind off sex."

Steve knelt beside the electronic safe,

studying the controls. Then he suddenly pulled out a screwdriver and ripped the digital display box from the safe. He grabbed red and green wires and sparked them together, and the safe clicked open. "Presto."

He pulled out the DVD player-recorder that was inside the safe. "Good. Go over to Mayor Lundquist's computer and see if you can find how they kept the disappearances secret," Gunter said. He pressed play.

Gunter, Steve, and Garzia listened. "People are disappearing on New Harmony Space Station. These disappearances seem to be random. We are unable to find any correlation of gender, race, class, or occupation in the victims."

"Scientists on board have noticed a spike in temperature that seems to be related to the disappearances. Immediately before disappearing, reports indicate that the victim's mind seems to go blank. No one has ever come back or been found. One person was reportedly feeling ill and reported to the medical ward. While being monitored, the patient experienced a dramatic increase in libido and reportedly wanted to take off all his clothes. He claimed to have seen naked women running around on the walls of New Harmony. No one else sensed or saw anything. Then he stared into space and suddenly vanished from the medical ward."

"We thought initially that the male physiology, driven by hormones, might be somehow triggering the disappearances. However, soon, women began disappearing. First, they felt sick. A spike in temperature soon followed, then the blank stares, the rise in libido, and reports of seeing people running, jumping, and bouncing from the floors to the walls and over railings. These nude people are always of the opposite sex of the victims."

"A call to the nearest spaceship in the vicinity requesting help has been transmitted. They will come to investigate. Captain Gunter Faber, a fine African captain with an excellent record, captains the Conestoga. Hopefully, we won't lose too many people before they arrive. The rise in the entire city's temperature continues to be a concern."

"We do know a mysterious meteor storm passed over the space station immediately before the disappearances began. Perhaps the station's hull was compromised, allowing the entrance of something to the city. Our scientists indicate that the New Harmony Space Station was pierced by space debris."

"A meteor," said Steve.

"Chondrite. Chondrite dominates the class of stony meteorites. That's probably what hit New Harmony. And at the speed all that space debris was traveling, there is no way this space station should have survived."

Steve was still clicking computer keys, watching the laptop screen. "Even with their shields?"

Gunter added quietly, "There was no shield capacity left after the first thirty minutes of the storm."

Garzia said, "A miracle."

"Regular, old-fashioned miracle," said Steve. "Like on Earth."

"Then why are half of the people dead on this space station?" Gunter asked.

"They are not exactly dead," Maria corrected. "We don't know exactly where they are. They may still be alive."

"Where?" Gunter said loudly, looking around.

Steve stopped searching the mayor's computer. "I'd like to second that request. Where exactly are they, Maria?"

"Another thing," Gunter added, "Why didn't the people panic when everyone started disappearing?"

"I can't explain that, sir. I can tell you that no there was no spike of activity in the flight port logs. No one tried to leave New Harmony. Very strange. I'd be out of here in a nano-sec if I knew the space station had been contaminated."

After clicking around, Steve said, "Look

here, Maria. 'New Harmony Space Station has a high number of people who have contracted a nonlethal virus. Contaminated personnel remain quarantined in their quarters until further notice. Standard quarantine period is two weeks.'"

"Enough time for us to be called, sir."

"Enough time to let the contaminant spread throughout the ship," Gunter replied solemnly.

Gunter began to fantasize about sex. He shook his head as if to toss out the distracting thoughts. His vision of her first appeared when he entered Borough #1. She glided over the walls in the nude, running as if the walls were floors, and stopped in front of him. She ran straight across his path, a foot away from him and up the opposite wall, standing there like some kind of gecko. She was barefoot, each pedicured toe painted in a different color – gold on her big toe, turquoise, black, blue, and pink. She stayed glued perpendicular to the New Harmony's light blue walls. Her heavy white breasts jiggled, hanging downward, as she stared.

He wanted to 69 her and kiss her bushy brunette triangle of pussy hair. Gunter wanted to squeeze her buttocks. She ogled him shamelessly. She ran her hands up and caressed her breasts, pinched her nipples, and licked her pink lips. She teased. She smiled slowly as if she experienced a sudden rush of attraction for him. Her slender thighs and legs tapered gently up to her wider hips, smaller waist, and those lovely white breasts, hanging like fruit. Her loneliness reached out to him.

She oozed power and control. They had something in common, a shared worldview. Gunter always finished things, did the job, and delivered the goods. So did she. He didn't understand it. None of it made sense, but Gunter knew she never started anything without finishing it. And now that he and she met, who knows what would happen? His fighting instincts kicked in and he rejected the beautiful apparition from his mind. But each time she came back stronger. She knew exactly what he wanted, his desires and needs. He refused to mention anything about this event to his crew. They had to tough it out, kick butt, resolve the mayhem, and not give in to it – or her, regardless of how wondrous this strange woman's physical charms were.

They belonged together because no world belonged to them.

"Captain? Captain Gunter Faber!" said Garzia, loudly.

Gunter shook his head, "Yes."

"You see a unicorn or something?" Steve yelled after running over and shaking Gunter.

"No. No unicorn," Gunter smiled and laughed. "You think I'd see a unicorn stuck out here in a floating space city, under the siege of aliens or some other space –"

"Space microbe, sir," said Garzia cautiously.

Gunter walked to over Mayor Lundquist's desk and started to put the DVD player-recorder on the desk. "I was trying to remember if I'd ever heard of any other case like this."

"Vampires." Garzia followed him, pulling out her toolkit to take his vitals. "Elevated testosterone. Higher temperature than normal."

Gunter thought again about leaving the only information they had on the problem. He put the DVD recorder-player inside his pocket. Then he took it out. "Here, Garzia. You're the scientist. You hold on to this."

"Sure, sir."

"She's right, Gunter. Vampires, according to legend, have the ability to hypnotize their prey, sexually, before biting."

Gunter looked about angrily, "You two are saying I've been bitten by something?"

"No. No," said Steve, as he moved around the room looking for clues.

"Besides, last time I heard of the genre, vampires could be seen not by mirrors but by everyday people," he pointed out. "You and Steve should have seen it."

"Correct, sir," Garzia said. "It's not a vampire – in the true sense."

Steve lifted a painting from the wall directly opposite to Mayor Lundquist's desk. He studied the back of the picture frame. "Of course, other legends suggest hallucination, subconscious desires brought to the surface."

"Succubus in the case of males, incubus for females. Creatures, negative angels that have sex with sleeping men and women," concluded Garzia.

"Look who's talking about sex now!" Steve chortled.

"Shut up, Steve. I mean it," Gunter roared. "We have a job and we're going to do it!"

"You are awake, Gunter," Steve said, becoming more serious. "So –"

"That's true," Garzia added. "But higher environmental temperatures and higher body temperature, added to the rise in sexual hormones, can give rise to sleep conditions."

"That's way too much science for me, Garzia." Steve put the wall painting back on the wall.

"I'm just saying staring blankly might be classified as sleep."

"Let's go see if the entire city is asleep," Gunter ordered.

Gunter, Steve, and Garzia reached a quad path. "We'll split up to speed the search," Gunter said. "Steve, you take Borough District #5 since you love the rich and famous. Garzia, you take Borough District #4, the upper middle class. I'll take Borough District #3, middle class. Keep your communicators open at all times, no matter what. Is that clear?"

"Yeah," Steve said, pulling out his gun.

"Yes, sir," replied Maria.

"We meet back here at 05:00; that's two hours from now. Then we'll all go in to Borough #2, which holds the arena-sporting complex. If there is any place things have happened, it'll be in Borough #2, but we cannot skip the other boroughs. We have to confirm our suspicions."

The three crewmembers of the Conestoga headed down the lit paths toward their respective boroughs. Gunter Faber started down the hallway toward Borough #3. He expected to meet some people, but no one was out walking. He entered one set of quarters after another and found them all the same. Empty. Frozen in time. Lived in to the very last moment before the residents disappeared. It reminded him of Pompeii, the ancient Roman city that was buried by a volcano. Dishes full of food, cups filled with fermenting wine, music playing, video visions playing movies on loops, or stations off the air. Clothes strung about. One room showed evidence of a man and a woman dressing for a ball. Tuxedo, white shirt, black pants, and spit-shined shoes laid out on the bed for him; lacy, pink ball gown, corsage, and spit-shined black flats, on the bed for her.

They were all the same. Libraries empty. Books dropped by people who disappeared while reading them. Computers still on, some in the middle of checking out DVDs, books, or old archives. Stacks of books waiting to be taken down to the library stacks retrieval from library tables. Toilets unflushed, tissue paper dropped where people might have been completing their required functions. All over the space city, things quit in mid-cycle, nothing completed. Beginnings of books never moved past page one.

Inside a large store, Gunter smelled something terribly burning. He ran toward the odor and found several loaves of bread burning in the oven. Products dropped when people vanished littered the walkways. Grocery carts half-full, full, and barely full were left in the middle of aisles, waiting for the people to return.

He went to the magazine aisle to see if any news talked about the disappearances. No mention of anything except a virus keeping a large number of people indoors.

"That confirms how they covered it up," Gunter thought. "No wonder there were no panicked departures registered on the flight port computers." Gunter's eyes moved down on the magazine and news rack methodically, looking for something, anything, that might explain the storm, the so-called virus. He began to flip through the pages of women's magazines. "Parents telling their children they couldn't play must have been rough," he thought. He flipped and saw a beautiful woman – like the one he saw in his visions. The woman appeared almost lifelike but nude, wearing only tiger-striped flats. Lovely straight brunette hair. He stared at her face when the picture moved.

He shook his head. Then he realized he was nude. Standing nude at the magazine rack. In fact, all the noise and business of people assaulted Gunter's ears. Suddenly before him, he saw several hundred people walking about the shop, nude, hand in hand, each one coupled off with the opposite sex. He shook his head, hoping to stop the vision.

In his youth, he had once visited a nudist camp, simply to broaden his experience. It had helped Gunter's awareness of humanity. In space training, they said, "Maybe we'll find people who don't believe in wearing clothes. We must prepare for anything. Clothing makes the human body sinful, and when people are nude, they realize how beautiful people really are. Equality, sharing, and understanding that we are all from the same lot come about from nudism." So Gunter didn't react in such a great shock about the nudity. He reacted to the fact that they were not shopping for food!

Her voice whispered out to him, "It's okay. You're safe. You don't need to struggle for food here." She came up to him, her high breasts full in soft ivory-pink color, like in his earlier visions. "All you need is love here." She came close to Gunter and embraced him. She kissed him. Gunter's feelings of loneliness surfaced. "I understand. We – you and I are a pair. Partners."

"Yes," she cooed. She laid her head on his shoulder and Gunter smelled her. She smelled like sunshine and roses. It reminded him of being outdoors gardening when he was a child. His grandma fell ill one day. She asked him to tend to her roses. He watered them for her and at some point acquired the love for flowers, which he had to suppress around boys and men.

"You can love gardening and flowering again, Gunter." She moved back and locked her wide blue eyes on his. Her nipple-length wavy hairdo covered her huge tits on each side. She took Gunter's hand and led him over to the reading area by the magazine rack. She led him to a small loveseat Gunter didn't remember seeing when he arrived. But it could have been there. His focus was on finding answers. She laid back. Her body fit perfectly and left enough legroom for Gunter's height to lie on top of hers.

The woman pursed her lips for a kiss and energy went out, pink lines to his black lips. He kissed her, a virtual kiss, a cyber-kiss. Only this world was as real as the other world. She kissed him before they physically kissed.

"Yes," she cooed. "Many ways exist to experience love. You only know a few, Gunter Faber."

Gunter said, "I want you so bad. I can't control myself."

"Men and women don't mate with inappropriate partners in this place. I am your perfect mate, Gunter."

"My perfect mate," Gunter said, slowly

removing his clothes, almost like a robot. He struggled to wonder what was happening to his body on the other side, back in the real New Harmony Space City.

"Yes. Each of us has a double. Inside." She caressed her breasts, moved her brunette straight hair from her nipples, aching, pinching upward. "Of the opposite sex, our true mate. What we secretly desire. Merging. Caring, loving, friendship, unbreakable bond of togetherness and love. You cannot resist."

"That's a lot for a man to swallow."

"There is no swallowing of love; you and I are love. Our togetherness assures harmony, peace, cooperation in the living. I am your Anima."

Gunter moved naked toward his Anima. "The female consciousness of my soul."

Gunter entered her warm, hot body. Her presence resisted him and held him. He didn't put all his weight on her as he began to move inside her wet warm cunt. Plowing. Drilling. Pushing. Pounding. He touched her gently. He did not want to harm her. His heart felt intertwined and connected in a thousand ways.

Gunter finally disappeared and reappeared in the second New Harmony Space Station. In the back of his mind, he heard faint voices.

"Gunter? You there? This is Steve checking in at 04:00. Maria, can you reach Gunter? I can't. Checking in at 04:00."

"Maria Garzia. Gunter, it's me, Garzia! Where are you?!" she shouted. "Are you okay? I've found everything in disarray in Borough #4. In the stores especially, no one present. Their quarters are like Pompeii."

"Maria, like Pompeii, that's what I was thinking. Just like Pompeii," Steve agreed. "Except there are no bodies around."

"I know, Steve, only the artifacts of how they lived right before the moment they disappeared. I found a couple's porno DVD playing on a loop, K-Y Jelly out, and a vibrator buzzing. Gunter, if you can hear me, listen. Listen!" Garzia said, "I found a young woman's diary. It said, 'A young man came to me this evening again. He came the evening before. He seemed to float through the walls. He wasn't there one moment and then he's there the next. He knows so much about me. I was in awe of his physical beauty, sure. I am only eighteen and unmarried. This guy practically read my thoughts. He told me he would return and on the third night, we'd go somewhere beautiful. I told him I can't go, but as I write this, knowing tonight, now is the third —'"

"Maria, is that it?!" Steve said anxiously.

"That's it, Steve. Gunter! Yes, Steve, she

never finished her entry. She disappeared. Her pen simply dropped where she was holding it!"

"Wow!" Steve didn't say anything. "Same thing here. I need to tell you though, Gunter, Maria. I can't account for ten minutes of my time. I must have been standing here at this fundraiser. All the fine wine, steak, oysters, cuisine vegetables left on so many tables. It's the weirdest thing I've seen. Fresh food, Garzia! I know I went to drink a glass of red wine and – how long can it take to take one drink of wine? Ten minutes?"

"You were there, Steve. On the other side, like Gunter probably is right now. Steve, we need to get together and find him. I'm second in command. That's an order, Steve!"

Maria and Steve's chatter drifted in and out of his consciousness. Gunter kept fucking his Anima on the loveseat next to all the magazines. He wanted to be very patient and understanding, allowing space for her to achieve her goals in helping him. The wisdom of his other half amazed him. He wanted to bring them closer, as close as possible. He accepted her, his Anima. He loved her. Their worldviews enabled them to see a mutual path. But still, something made him want to get back to the real world.

Gunter finished having sex with the gorgeous woman.

"I'll visit you again," she cooed.

"I'll be waiting," Gunter lied.

She smiled as if she knew his thoughts and it was a game. "I'll come for us."

Gunter put his clothes on and suddenly appeared in the magazine aisle. Immediately he heard Garzia running toward him, saying, "I found him, Steve. In the magazine aisle!"

"I'm one aisle over, Maria! I'll be right there." Steve rounded the corner to the magazines. "Gunter!"

Gunter smiled. "Maria, Steve. I'm glad you didn't get pulled in and lost."

"You didn't answer our check at 04:00?"

"What time is it now?"

"05:00."

"We're late. We have to check Borough #2. I have some ideas about how to solve this."

They ran into Borough #2. "Our best place to look is in the arena."

"Why the arena?" said Garzia.

Steve replied, "Because that's where most people would have disappeared."

They entered the arena. Hundreds of empty chairs sat as an audience of zero waited. All their artifacts, programs, purses, books, binoculars, and even some hearing aids were abandoned, dropped right where the people sat. "I bet if I take a reading, all the hormones and temperatures would be off the charts." Garzia started walking around, heading up to the empty stage.

Steve agreed. "My thought exactly, Garzia."

"Steve, how much time did you lose in Borough #5?"

"About ten minutes," he said cautiously. "I only remember snippets."

Garzia walked around measuring for different atmospheric conditions.

"I remember. That's our Anima."

"She is my Anima."

"Only your Anima, buddy," Gunter said.

"She was so fucking hot. Hey, Garzia hasn't lost any time."

"She's a scientist. She won't allow herself to believe in anything other than what she can see and feel."

"I see. What do I do when my Anima comes back?"

"Agree with her. Go with the flow."

"Is that how you came back?"

Gunter nodded. "We had great sex."

"From what little I remember, I'd say the same."

"Findings confirmed. Whatever it is – microbe, virus – there's a whole sea full of it in here. My conclusion is those people are still here," she said standing on the stage.

"I agree, Garzia," Gunter shouted. "Men see their Anima and women see their Animus in Second New Harmony Space Station now."

Garzia said as she walked back, "Somehow the virus or meteor made them more susceptible to their own subconscious?"

Steve asked, "Why haven't you had any visions, Maria?"

"I did when we took off our helmets. I just didn't want to admit it. You boys would have said I was being hysterical."

"Why do they parkour around the walls?" Steve asked.

"Easier to get your attention, I guess," Maria said, back with Steve and Gunter.

"In that other city, New Harmony 2, different rules exist," Gunter revealed. "No need for food, drink, clothes."

"An alternate universe."

Maria countered, "Their alternate universe."

"Everyone left on New Harmony will leave with us," Gunter ordered. "Garzia, you scan to find how many people are left on board. Steve, you go to the intercom –"

Steve was staring blankly ahead,

unresponsive. Gunter tried slapping him, hard across the jaw. Steve's eyes opened wider.

"His testosterone is rising. Temperature is five degrees above normal and rising. His heart is racing. It's like he's having sex!"

Gunter punched Steve. Steve's face moved jerkily to the left, but he did not break his stare. "Steve! Steve Volk! I order you to stand down!"

Garzia kept measuring his vitals. "Sir, we've got to get him out of this arena!"

"You take his left arm. We'll drag his ass out of here." Gunter and Maria carefully leaned Steve at an angle and began dragging him backwards out of the sports complex when they suddenly rushed forward – without Steve.

"What?"

"Steve!" Maria Garzia shouted. She pulled out her instruments, measuring the surroundings. "No life forms found in the arena! And, sir, no life forms found anywhere on New Harmony – except two!"

"Damn! Our only hope is to get back to our space suits."

"I agree, sir. Our space suits may protect us."

They began to walk out of the arena when a beautiful strange vision appeared before Gunter Faber. He saw the entire Second New Harmony Space Station engaged in a mass orgy. Man on woman. Woman on man. Everyone coupled off and was having every kind of sex imaginable. Mayor Lundquist, naked, fucking some black girl doggy style. They were alive, but....

Then Gunter sees her, his Anima partner floating – coming closer. The woman of his dreams.

Garzia, reading her instruments, said, "Rise in testos –" She pulled Gunter by the arm hard, "Faster, run faster, Gunter."

"Okay. Thanks, Garzia!"

They ran out of the arena and the door shut behind them.

"To the space dock, Garzia." Both ran as fast as they could, their silver uniforms blending in with the bright walkway lights inside the huge floating city. Gunter and Maria ran back the way they came when Maria stopped at the quad path – four paths, each leading to a different Borough district.

"The temperatures are higher down our clearest path back, sir. We have to go another way. Follow the lowest temperature!"

"What way?"

Garzia raised her instruments at the quad path before them. She pointed, "Borough District #3."

"I'm all for the middle class, Garzia."

Both Gunter and Garzia ran as fast as

they could, when the lights in the hallway blinked on and off suddenly. "Power shortage. Do a reading on our locators, Garzia."

"Completing right now," she panted, still running full speed. "All spacesuits accounted for – for now."

"For now?"

"The temperature is rising in the space dock."

"Hurry, Garzia." Gunter barreled down the walkways of the city faster and faster, leaving Garzia sprinting slower behind him. "Move it! Move it! Garzia!"

Gunter turned back every minute and shouted to Garzia to keep up. They ran faster than they ever had before, far faster than they had during training. Gunter hit the corners with the precision of a basketball player doing sprints. Garzia held on to the corners of the walkways to propel her faster toward the space dock.

"We're there, Garzia! We made it."

"Yes, s –"

"Garzia!" Gunter turned around to find his scientist had vanished.

Gunter entered the space dock and felt woozy. He struggled against the sleepiness and fought it off long enough to put on his space suit and helmet. Then he felt better. He pressed the undocking button and allowed the dock to pressurize. The female computer voice said, "No contamination.

You are free to leave."

Gunter entered his ship, the Conestoga, and took over the controls. He set the autopilot for the next nearest space station. Then he called the High Council for Flight Corp. He rested in his silver suit in the cockpit, alone, thinking about what he would say to the High Council. How to explain it?

"That's all I can remember," said Gunter in a serious tone. "I tried very hard to bring my crew back. We tried to resolve the problem on the New Harmony City Space Station. I don't think there was anything anyone could have done."

"Are you sure you can't remember anything else?" said a white older woman on the High Council.

"Yes. That's what happened."

The Peruvian councilwoman said, "A flash meteor storm crashed into the New Harmony Space Station, and 3,440 people on board started dying."

The Chinese councilman said, "Shriveling up."

"Then disappearing," added the German councilman.

"You disappeared into another level of the space station and there you met these...beings."

"Who took over your mind and tried to prevent your return."

Silence.

"Only I escaped." Gunter lowered his head but then held it high. "That's what happened. I recommend New Harmony City be quarantined immediately."

The Jewish guy asked, "Can you tell us why only you escaped?"

"I don't know." Gunter hesitated, "You must understand when something like this happens and you're the only survivor, you don't know what to make of it. Faith. Luck. Fate. Love. Acts of the goddesses and gods." Gunter shrugged. "I'd like to think I gained a better understanding of myself through this crisis."

"And have you?" asked the Peruvian woman.

"Regardless of our skills and no matter how excellent our training, the goddesses and gods enable us to start things and finish things. That is what I've learned."

5 DOLLHOUSE EROTICA

Satisfaction crossed her lips. Her high cheekbone features became more animated, appearing and disappearing as she opened and closed her mouth. The nineteen-year-old beauty's mouth formed O shapes of various sizes. I imagined each O size musically toning an "Ah," "Ohh," "Ahhhh." Morrjodi's mysterious black eyes clinched tight against the reality of her bedroom. Her shiny oil-black hair spread out on her pink pillow. Her bangs swept to the side. Her perfect lifeguard body undulated on her white bed sheets, and the King size bed rocked gently up and down, matching her humping hips, forcing her fingers to plunder her wet pussy over and over, again. I stood transfixed. In my own bedroom, across the narrow alley, I watched her through the outside darkness that arrived two hours ago, eight p.m. Morrjodi and I attended different colleges. Morrjodi must have known her lit bedroom made an excellent peep show, and I'm a horny guy twenty years old. I would look.

Tonight there were no shadows across her heart. I shared her open celebration of lust and possible love, although I didn't want it to be love for another. Morrjodi, who some said was a witch already, was my love. Her butterscotch-tanned hips rose high off the bed jostled her lovely middling breast, to and fro, pushing against one another. When she began undressing one hour ago, I randomly walked to retrieve a love book, the story of Johann Goethe. I saw her blinds surprisingly raised, the gauzy curtains drawn as usual. Unable to resist her, finally revealed charms, I dropped my red running shorts to my kneecaps and started masturbating.

My cock, fully extended seven inches in seconds, was hard. Some opportunities come only once in a lifetime. I had proof now, witches masturbated. This proof of her intimate humanity made me less afraid to approach her. Maybe I'd even ask her out. Either way, tonight, I am determined not to miss this, one, Morrjodi's passionate bed dance. When her body rose again high off the white bed sheets, I knew this was the moment, our moment. If inside the Irish cutie, I'd groaned loudly and say, "I'm coming, Morrjodi!" Quickly, I pulled up my shorts and shot copious wads of hot jism into my shorts, not even caring if some of it dripped onto my bedroom carpet. I had to see the very end. Morrjodi lay still, quiet, monitoring her breathing, settling down back to reality. She opened her eyes. She pulled her sopping hand from her pussy and gave in to the irresistible impulse to smell her own love juices. Then she licked her hand.

Suddenly, she turned looked about her room, down pass the foot of her bed to her stereo systems, to the left where her three-tiered open dollhouse sat against the wall, to her right at her alarm clock, before viewing the window. An angry expression overtook her pretty face and she rose, ignoring her nakedness, and came toward the window. Her naked V split by one thin hot line slipping and sliding in her own sex fluids, her clit still protruding. Morrjodi offered me a matching obscene gesture to go with the "fuck you" formed by her mouth as her bedroom window blinds slammed down cutting off my vision of her.

I shrugged my shoulders and began wiping my cum off my thighs and legs. I walked toward the bathroom when my phone rang. I tossed my soaked red running shorts, dashed back to answer my cell. "Unknown Call." I answered it. "Hello, this is Flint."

"Still want to see my bedroom, Pervert!"

I didn't know how to answer. "I—I." Before I blinked a second time, I stood naked from the waist down, semi-hard, love fluid still on my sensitive cock. My white, short-sleeve cotton shirt with black trim covering half my buttocks and half my sex. "What?" I also began to feel very strange.

"Yes, witches make horny love to themselves," Morrjodi snarled, standing two inches away from me in her red Longnecks Sports Grill T-shirt. Her straight oil-black hair touched her shoulder and formed curves around her neck and chin. She pointed, "We also listen to music, watch some cable, and use to play with dollhouses."

"Listen, Morrjodi—I'm—I'm sorry." Normally, I stood my eye-to-her forehead. Now, we were eye-to-eye.

"Too late. You peeped me," she smiled in a wicked way, lifted the hem of her red Sports Grill T-Shirt, "N.A.K.E.D."

It was snarl-to-jocks smile she often gave out at the beach—especially the jocks who faked like they were drowning, when they knew fully well how to swim. I didn't see what the big deal was. Lots of girls got naked on the Internet. "Ok. I didn't have to look—." I felt an apology might get me a teleported back to my own apartment. Otherwise, I'd have to run down her house stairs nude, feeling all strange and weird, my shirt now feeling way too big somehow, and who knows what her father and mother might say.

She looked at my eye-to-her chiseled nose now. "No. No. You wanted to be in my bedroom." She walked toward her dollhouse, her tight butt lifting the red T-shirt in an up and down beat. "You can just stay in my bedroom forever." She turned around, didn't blink, and her entire eyes went black. She waved her forefinger from me to the dollhouse.

Now, I realized what the weird feeling meant, as I found Morrjodi growing taller and looking stronger and bigger by the second. My T-shirt formed this white covering on the carpet under me. I, now, stood bare-ass naked. When I realized her balled up, discarded white sock, stuffed inside her white and pink gym shoes met my eye, I got really scared. I heard the loud echoing sound of Morrjodi's frilly laugh bouncing off the walls. I put my hands over my ears. The carpet thumbed under my feet shaking the ground. She came over me, and I saw right up her huge pussy slot, still open, gaping from sex. Her beautiful musky sex scent covered the room and wafted down, sent my mind whirling in pleasure. Her hand reached down, the huge red-painted fingernail that enveloped me. I rose in her hand. She brought me close to her, eye-to-eye. "If you can survive having sex with Barbie, I'll return you to your room."

Morrjodi turned around and my blond hair flew back in the breeze. She fondled my tiny dick with her pinkie finger. "You have to make it to Barbie's bedroom on her third floor." She held me by my tiny waist, my back to her and facing the three-tiered dollhouse. "First floor is her study and bathroom; second floor is her living room, I call it the music room. The entire house is only 475-inches tall, 16-inches wide, and 34.75-inches long. So I'm sure you'll have enough time to play in her wooden dollhouse."

A high-pitch laugh blasted through the Barbie's dollhouse and shook the walls, a small painting of a horse with a yellow saddle white background fell off the wall. Morrjodi placed me in one of the brown wooden chairs with green seats, at a light brown table. A stove before me seemed real. The oven doors opened out. Four burners on the left side and large cooking space on the right. Behind the study, a bathroom, held a pink rim tube, toilet covered in yellow top, and large mirror over the sink. The floor checkered light black and hot pink tiles. An escalator of gray steps moved up on the left side and down on the right. I stood up to explore the place as Morrjodi smiled wickedly. Her huge face and body growing smaller as she retreated to her bed. I watched the sweet hot line under her sex retreating further away in seconds. Loud music from Angela Laving blared.

"What is that loud music!" the feminine voice using a southern drawl said, descending from the down escalator.

I didn't want to believe she was real.

Barbie put both hands over her ears. "Honestly, why did I get placed in a house where a nympho witch girl likes loud music?" Barbie went to the right wall near a white large four-panel window and snapped her fingers and the dollhouse closed completed. We were walled in, in silence.

"Thank you, Barbie." I said in relief. "I thought my eardrums might liquefy."

"Liquefy?" She giggled demurely. "Liquefy. Never heard that before about music."

"I'm sorry. But—I." I turned back toward the wall and front door, where Morrjodi's room used to be. "I need to visit your third floor, have sex with you, and then I'll be out of your business—forever!" I smiled cautiously and nodded toward the up escalator.

"What do you think I am, Flint! A whore!" She pointed to her 39-inch breasts tied securely in a black cinching tank and a lilac wrap sweater. Below, she wore a red gypsy skirt and wedge sandals.

"No—I—certainly not!" I stammered. Barbie dimensions made me happy. Any woman who measured 39D-23-30 offered everything a man needed for happiness and ultimate joy. "Where's Ken?" I tried to change the subject.

She cast her eyes downward and went to look in the oven. I sat back down and I noticed somehow the house lacked room, because Barbie's sweet smelling behind moved two inches from my face. In fact, I could see right through the flimsy red material. She wore white panties.

She pulled out a tray of cinnamon rolls, "They're good and hot!" The tray clanged on the four burner. "Oops! Ouch!" She licked her fingers. She reached into the drawer on the right side of the stove for a spatula. She scooped it up and turned back around to face me. "Want one?"

My eyes stared at her huge nipples. Her nipples were going to make some baby fat and plump because I imagined the easy flow of milk from those two inch nips. Her nipples pressed against her black cinching tank. "Sorry. I got distracted." I reached for one.

"It's okay. I stopped wearing a bra long ago." She put a cinnamon roll on her own plate and sat down. "Bra's chaff. Although I wear one in my music room, lots of girls are burning their bras nowadays," as she stuffed her face with the hot cinnamon roll.

"Very good." I nodded, and the combined smell of Barbie's rose water perfume and cinnamon roll made me settle down and relax. I didn't have to fuck Barbie in her bedroom as soon as possible. I might enjoy her company. She didn't seem like the airhead most people made her out to be—so far anyway. "If you're not dating Ken, why don't we date?"

"Mmmmm. This is good. I've out-done myself." She swallowed. Clasped her hands in front of her, dropped her chin over her hands and eyed me carefully. "Because I don't know you."

"You know my name is Flint."

"Surely, a girl has to know more than a half-naked boy's last name before she makes love." She touched me on my arm.

I felt her basked in the knowledge of her power. She had me in her house. I watched her eyeing me with smug delight. But then again, I felt a strange calm comfort around her. "I blurted out a confession. "OK. I watched Morrjodi masturbating in her bedroom tonight. That is why I'm here." I forced myself to remain calm. "I...if you and I make love in your bedroom, she'll let me go back home."

Barbie walked around to my chair and hugged me. "That's sweet." She went into the bathroom and I heard her tinkling on the toilet. "Who is Morrjodi?" Then there was a flush. I heard her washing her hands. She came out and pulled her chair over closer to me. I sat facing the same way, but Barbie sat next to me facing the stove now.

"Morrjodi—Morrj—She owns this house."

Barbie stared at me. She looked closely at my wild spiked blond hair. I saw her almost measuring my chest, now that she'd hugged me. She pressed her arms around my biceps. "How tall are you? Come on stand up, Flint."

I rose. She placed her hand on my head. Then she moved it straight across to her head.

"I like a man who doesn't tower over me." She grabbed both my hands and spread my arms. "You look lost, Flint."

"I'm not lost. Morrjo—."

"All I know is she's a witch." She blinked both eyes at me.

I pulled Barbie close.

"Oh these breasts," she laughed out loud, "They do get in the way don't they?" She pressed me up against her chest harder. I felt her huge nipples hardening under the cinchy black top. Her nipples practically massaging my tits, and excited, I started extending below the waist.

"You're playing stick magic or I'm playing with fire!"

"Perhaps, it is a little of both." We started slow dancing.

"This will go a lot easier with some music." She said, "Let's go upstairs to my music room.

Upstairs in Barbie's living room, a full baby grand piano sat on the left. Her daybed couch of bright yellow on a wood frame to the right. In the middle, her music system, CD, DVD players, and flat wall screen covered the middle. A small bookcase holding a series of romance novel and short stories sat behind the daybed.

"Music always makes sex go better, don't you think, Flint."

Her southern drawl worked its magic. I began to develop deep feelings for Barbie. Normally, being a feminist, I hated Barbie. But it is obvious I've misjudged the girl.

"You have to get to know a girl before

you can judge her, my mom use to always say." An antebellum waltz of some sort came on.

The music intoxicated me. I don't know why. Maybe it was the scent of rose water on Barbie's skin. We came together and danced hand-to-hand, shoulder-to-shoulder, and face-to-face. "I totally agree." We spun around at a leisurely pace. "I dance pretty well for a half-nude man-clothed woman scenario."

"You do, Flint." She leaned back on my hand behind her.

I took the hint, dipped her, and planted a fiery kiss on her soft lips. Barbie responded with a hungry kiss of her own. Her kiss surprised me as it belied her outward calm. I pulled her back up and she pushed forward, pressing her heavy 39D breasts against me and took my lips with her moist mouth. Barbie's lips were more demanding the second time. She rose up on her tiptoes and devoured my mouth. We turned in a clockwise circle kissing as if our lives depended upon it. Suddenly, she broke our embrace.

"My! You sure know how to show a girl a good time, Flint." She fanned herself. A blush appeared on her cheeks. "A little music?" She nodded to the piano.

Barbie sat down on the piano. She patted the stool beside her.

I sat down and she began playing a

song from Casablanca. "Love this song, 'a kiss is but a kiss, a sigh is but a sigh.'" Then she broke the mood by playing fast 20s flapper song. Then she got up and danced like a flapper. She somehow put the music on auto. But the piano keys did not move like a player piano keys moved. Clearly, Barbie's jubilant and capricious nature was emerging. I clapped my hands and my sex swelled to complete hardness. Barbie's flirting eyes darted from my eyes to my stiff sex and back to my chest. I wanted this girl. I wanted to do animal things to her. Make her listen to the wet sounds of sex and the drip of ice melting. I listened to the music as she danced.

Her Gypsy skirt rising higher and higher on her thighs as she held the thin fabric. She infused ravenous desire in me. I only hoped she felt the same as she ripped off her skirt and dance in her white nylon panties. Panties stretched so tight across her sex; her clit protruded and invited my tongue to involuntary lick and swirl in my mouth. I came to her and kissed her again, first on the hollow of her ivory neck. Then I possessed her mouth, but for a second, before she possessed mine. The ambience of sex filled the air. Her musky and floral scents and my sweaty skin drove our passions.

I lay Barbie down on the daybed.

She heaved her great breasts forward,

almost coming out from her top. "Oh, I don't do this often with men named Flint."

"Pretend I'm Ken." My hands were all over her body, caressing her legs, thighs, belly, and back.

She reached down and touched my sex with her delicate warm hands. "I don't like Ken anymore." She panted.

"Pretend I'm the man of your dreams!" I groaned and placed myself on top of her.

"Don't think I'm a whore, Flint."

"I don't. I won't."

She unbuckled her purple sweater wrap. She raised her black cinch top. She left on her bra, but her heavy breasts fell freer over her chest. I imagined the moment when her breasts spread like milk for the longest time all over my chest. I wanted to lick her breasts. I went down and licked her breasts through the bra material. I started from the outside and licked inward, in circles. Tighter and tighter, I made the circle until Barbie panted.

"Those circles make my sex smaller inside."

I sucked her expansive sensitive breast flesh into my lips. Each kiss, placing one puckered suck in circles, smaller and smaller, as I neared Barbie's two-inch nipples.

"OK. It's okay."

"What's OK, Barbie," I managed to say

between sucking both nipples, searching for the milk of her desire.

"That I'm a whore in the bed." She pressed her own hand down between us. I felt her circling her own clit. Her groin grew hotter and she pressed up to solve her urgent needs. I humped down, pushing my stiffness into the V of her sex and groves of her busy fingers.

"I'm coming!" Barbie screamed.

"Come for me, Baby." I commanded her.

I touched her lightly, but continued to suck her gentle soft breasts through the bra. She calmed down and recovered.

"I'm going to get married one day. Then I won't fuck visitors sent here."

"You've had other guys sent, made small to visit?"

"Plenty." Barbie gazed into the pink ceiling. "From as far back as I can remember, in my adult life. You see Flint, Morrjodi and I use to be best friends forever." She sighed.

Caressing a woman seriously in need of a friend didn't match my M.O. Sure I had to get back to my world. I could try to help Barbie in her world.

Barbie lay on her daybed. Her disheveled appearance made her cute not slutty. "I don't know where we went wrong. We use to play together all the time. Of course, we didn't do anything but girl stuff. You know."

"What happened?"

"That's just it, Flint. I don't exactly know."

"Boys."

Barbie shook her head. "More than Boys. It's sex. I believe she wants what I have, the boobs, the money, easy life."

My tremendous desire dropped below my waist. But, my heart opened up to Barbie. "Life provides different path to everyone."

"I carry the weight of my relationship with Ken." She waved her gentle hand in the air, "My reputation is tainted. Some think I'm a slut. Others say I'm an airhead." She began to sob.

"There—there, Barbie." I consoled her. I rolled over and took the dangerous side of the daybed. The side without a back. One jolt of her great breasts and I'd be tossed to the Music room floor. "I think Morrjodi's struggling with the same issues. She's a lifeguard and some people think she's there as eye-candy."

"Eye candy! Saving someone's life is hard work." Barbie batted her eyelids at me.

"Not just that." I paused. "How to explain it? What happens to a girl the second, the minute she isn't saving someone's neck? Her astounding beauty makes her look like an ornament or something."

Barbie nodded her head. I saw the fearful clarity sinking in. Then she moved to sit up and I crashed my naked ass to the hard floor.

"That's it. That's when she first pulled away from me." She closed her eyes to bring back that moment and it played out before us in the music room. Morrjodi's mother scolding her for playing with her dollhouse all the time.

"I'm done with Chemistry, History, and Literature, mom."

"You must have something else to do."

"It's all done, mom. Honest!"

"You should go out and volunteer or something."

"I don't want to volunteer. I want to play with my imagination."

"Draw, write, play music, and take up ballet!"

"Those take time away from my studies!"

"I should never have bought you that dollhouse. It's evil."

"It's not evil!"

"I want you to participate in some clubs or groups in high school."

Barbie sniffled. "That's when Morrjodi first joined the Young Wiccans Club."

I was sitting naked cross-legged on the floor, listening. I felt something more than sexual desire though. I wanted to put my head in my hands, too, but that sent the wrong message. If I was going to get out of here, out of Barbie's world, and back into the real world, my world, I needed Barbie's help. Barbie's problem mirrored Morrjodi, in a strange way. Barbie, designed by the toy makers, is for girls doing outdoor things in the home. Girls don't have to go out into the real world, because Barbie, wonder girl, does it for them. I got up and sat next to Barbie on the daybed again. I put my arm around her shoulder. "And?"

Barbie crossed her pale arms across under her ample chest. She turned to face me. "I lost my best friend forever."

"Have you ever thought of studying Wicca?" I raised my left eyebrow, unsure if she'd take the bait. Actually, it wasn't bait. Just a way for her to do something in common with Morrjodi.

"I know Wicca already." She paused. "Sort of. I—I mean all women possess natural skills of Wicca. Women are naturals. We don't really have to study a bunch of books." She tossed her head back, moving her blonde hair behind her back. "That's why men call us witches when they get angry." She shrugged her shoulders.

"Then—you can connect again to Morrjodi." My eyes fell to Barbie's panty crotch involuntary. I wanted to embrace her and love her now as a friend. Perhaps, it was too soon. Maybe, I needed to let her simmer and solve the "best friend forever" problem longer. Conflicting emotions raged through me. It didn't make sense, I'm a feminist. What do I and Barbie have in common? Except the oppressive system that makes women and girls be things they are not. Barbie had a doll girlfriend, but who remembers her.

She has to be with Ken. If she's not with him, she doesn't really have a reason for existing. She's not recognized for the person inside, only her body outside. Hot body, huge breasts. Flawless makeup. Fashionable clothes. Home and things. Throw in a couple of children and a white picket fence and she'd be an invisible stay-at-home mom. Not a pleasant or rewarding thing for a future life, Barbie deserved more.

"You know, Flint. You're the first guy to sit down and just talk with me." She let a smoldering sexual smile cross her lips as her eyes dropped from my eyes to my growing cock. She twirled her right forefinger around strands of her golden locks. She uncrossed her arms and hugged me.

I was a sucker for hair courting females. "You know, Barbie," I waved my forefinger at her playfully, "I think you like me."

"You do!" she said drawing out the last word in her southern drawl.

I nodded. "I do." I pressed closer to her

hot body. I whispered, into her ear, "I'm thinking, you want to invite me upstairs."

"Wait." She got up and went to her closet behind the Grand Piano. She made a chagrin face. "Morrjodi sent so many bad guys here—to me." She opened the closet door.

I followed her. I say a hundred guys pictures hung inside tiny black-ringed frames on the wall. "This is my Bad Guy Behavior Wall."

"I—I can see that." I pointed to a few. "Yup. He's a jerk. And that guy—you don't even want to know all the evil things he'd did to girls." Although, I rubbed my chin, "their behavior has been exceptional this past year." I bobbed my head back and forth sideways thinking. "You—you changed them!"

"Yes, I did." Barbie agreed. "All their bad boy behavior is locked inside that little circle. Once that was extracted, they were rather nice boys actually." She added and smiled.

"You were going to put me there, too." I pointed into her closet of Boy Shame Behavior.

Barbie started an infectious gawffling laughter.

And I started laughing too.

"No, I wasn't." She turned and planted a hot kiss on my mouth.

My tongue traced circles around her

tongue. I gave myself freely to the passion of her kiss. She slammed the closet door. She embraced me with both arms. "I'm feeling horny now, Flint. Let's go upstairs."

In no time, we appeared upstairs in her bedroom. Her queen-sized bed took up most of the space. She faced the bed east to west, her headboard facing the right wall. Behind her bed, a small table holding a small lamp light for reading and five another collections of near-porn romance books. Behind that, a huge bookcase of more steamy romance books and erotica books like the Pearl, Kama Sutra for Women, and a smattering of sex books on female sexuality mixed into the columns bookcase paperbacks. "That's my midnight reading. Sometimes, even pretty girls get those urges down there."

"Down where?"

"You know," she drawled out. She sat down on the bed. On the opposite of her bed was a big screen television. "I've even recorded a few DVDs of myself masturbating."

"Masturbating where?"

She placed her hand gently over her sex, "My pussy."

"Don't say words that make me grow fonder, Barbie." I placed my hand on her naked thigh, inches away from her panty-covered pussy. I could feel heat emanating from that sacred fireplace between her legs. I leaned over and kissed Barbie's shoulder. Then I kissed her neck and the back of her shoulder. I lightly smoothed my hand down her back and let my fingers trace the inside of her panty waistband. I dipped a finger into her derriere cheek groove. I sighed. "I want you Barbie."

"OK. Here's how we do this." She pushed me back on my back. My hand still wedged between her buttocks. "I know you don't love me. You feel something for me." She pulled my hand out from her derriere and licked my finger. "Tell me what you feel for me, the woman, not the icon Barbie." She pointed to her chest. "Inside here." She pointed to her heart.

I stay laying down. I narrowed my eyes. "Wise and serene, beautiful and strong, Barbie loves life. Your strength does not mask your femininity. You can be playful or think seriously about the complex world. Your overwhelming beauty goes beyond huge heavy breasts, flawless makeup, and long sensuous legs. You're a serious expression of womanhood—once, a guy gets to know you inside," I cautioned, "not just inside your sex. Inside your soul. You love."

"You're saying that."

"Actually I am." I joked.

"You beast!" She lay on top of me, laughing, and smacking my arms playfully. "I'm going to make you pay for that by squeezing you hard everywhere that matters. She straddled my legs. I wondered when this would happen. Barbie wasted no time, smothering me in her hot kisses. Her tongue and lips sucked my tongue. She ran her tongue around my lips. My hands felt all over her back and neck, as I held her to me. I didn't want to let her go. She felt warm, and a little steamy dewy moisture appeared all over her skin. She let her full weight sit on top of my cock, and naturally, I grew harder and straighter. I reached down past her belly button and let my fingers dip beneath her panties until I found her sex. I rubbed up and down her pleasure groove making sure to take the growing moisture and massage it all along her sex and clit. I could tell by her sighs and heavy breathing, Barbie enjoyed our passionate embrace.

She whispered in my ear, "My bra comes off last." Then she tongued my ear and kissed my cheeks until her mouth found mine again. Her frisky humping motions turned my cock from hard to ultra-hard and a full expression of my raging desires. I wanted to dip into Barbie's sex like a river going over a waterfall and falling into a quiet stream below. I arched up. I pulled Barbie closer to me, as close as I could get with her 39D breasts massaging all over my hard nipples. Barbie didn't let her hands go idle. She showed her constant hungry desire for me by rubbing my sides and my chest and pushing her hands between us, down to my sex. She grabbed my cock and massaged it. She pulled my cock forward. Raising up a little, then she lay her full weight back down on my cock and slid up and down. Her flat belly fucking the underside of my penis, locking the surging liquid desire into my stiffness. I felt her lubricating under the manipulations of my hands inside her white panties.

"Let me take these off," Barbie said. She dismounted off me and shimmied down her panties to her ankles. She kicked off her panties, which rose in the air and fell onto my face. I held the skimpy damp garments and inhaled. I swear I grew another inch of hardness. I held out my arms. "Come, Barbie."

Barbie straddle my body again. "I'm going to miss you, Flint."

"Just call me whenever you want a visit." I replied.

She sat up her clit thrumming against my throbbing cock. Then she lifted her hips, while my hands held her waist and she engulfed my urgent need for passion.

The fact that her great breasts were real, her attitude saucy and her rowdy riding on top of my hard cock showed all sincerity assured me I'd be home in no time. The top of my desire felt the tingle tongue touch of her cervix kissing me. Barbie's warm body felt good. Her breasts bounced in her bra, and the added gravitational pull gave her an extra fuck motion when she sat down on my cock.

I reached up and massaged her two-inch nipples through her bra. I wanted her to spill all her milky breasts all over my face. I needed her to show me her fully nude body. I already saw the base of Venus' Hill grinding against my balls and sweaty crotch hairs. I knew we both neared the end, the epic merger of our new friendship. A sexual flush appeared all over Barbie's skin. She reached back both hands behind her back. "I'm coming! I'm coming, Flint!" she screamed out and gracefully the garment slid down her arms and she tossed it over somewhere, and lowered her boobs to my face smothering me in her soft succulent milky flesh globs and moved them around in large circles all over my chest. I groaned loud and shot several wads into her baby-maker pussy. I gave a soft sigh and arched up and came one more time, and we lay like that for several minutes.

"That was the best time I've had in years," she said.

"We should do it again," I replied to Barbie.

"I'll talk with Morrjodi."

After lying there talking about all kinds of things like meditation and spirituality, Barbie said, "It's late. You should be leaving."

"I don't—exactly know how to get home—" I stammered.

"I do." She winked at me and waved her left hand.

"Whoa!" I said, as I appeared back inside my room in front of the window. Morrjodi's curtains were drawn, her blinds down, but I suspected she was masturbating again. Oh well, you can't win them all. And at least I got to understand Barbie and fuck her. She's not a bad girl at all. She is actually a good girl.

AUTHOR'S NOTE

Readers: I want to expand a few of the stories to see where the characters can be explored further. If there are any of the stories that you would like to read more about again, I'd love to hear from you!

Visit my blog at www.ericresher.com

Join my newsletter for free exclusive previews
http://www.ericresher.com/in

Follow me on Twitter at
http://www.twitter.com/ericresher

Like my page on Facebook at
http://www.facebook.com/ericresher

Discover my books at major ebook retailers everywhere.